GASPAR BROWN

ADVENTURE 2

More Gaspar Brown Adventures

by

Hutton Wilkinson

GASPAR BROWN

AND THE

MYSTERY OF THE

SEMINOLE SPRING

ADVENTURE 2

HUTTON WILKINSON

Gaspar Brown and the Mystery of the Seminole Spring
© 2018 Hutton Wilkinson

Book design by Sue Campbell Book Design

ISBN 13: 978-1-7325653-0-2 (print)

For
Ruth

CONTENTS

PROLOGUE

FOR THE PAST THREE MONTHS THE STORY OF GASPAR BROWN, THE BOY BILLIONAIRE HAD THE GULF COAST of Florida abuzz. Whether it was the 500,000 acre Perdido Isle inheritance from his mother's mysterious great uncle Charles Munoz-Flores y Gaspar, or *La Rinconada*, his amazing house full of treasure the vast income attached to the land that people found hard to believe, was anyone's guess. Gaspar and his mother Elvira Brown had moved to Perdido Isle from their humble life in California shortly after learning about the inheritance from local Florida lawyer Peter Cawthorne. Although everyone was talking about the Browns' "good fortune", for Gaspar and his mom the magnitude of the reality of their riches was still sinking in.

La Rinconada was the jewel in Gaspar Brown's crown. But it was the income from 100,000 leased acres, as well as the rents from the two commercial "Main Streets" of the island's almost-twin towns of Calaluna and Llojeta, that provided the all important grease that made the squeaky wheels of young Gaspar's newly inherited empire turn. This massive income would soon come in handy to fund some of the boy billionaire's more creative projects.

Upon arrival at La Rinconada, Gaspar met his new best friend and sidekick, Alex Mendoza. Alex's parents, Felix and Angela, were the caretakers on the property. The Mendoza family lived in an apartment above the old stables and were happily on hand to help Gaspar and his mom, as they settled into their new life in Florida.

A new addition to La Rinconada's friendly staff was Margaret Stewart, who Gaspar had taken on as his official librarian. The library at La Rinconada was an important one … full of personal family archives as well as rare editions, portfolios of photographs, old maps, land surveys and a myriad of exceptionally interesting ephemera. Miss Stewart had been an old friend of Gaspar's great uncle Charlie, and had helped the old boy form the library, not only at La Rinconada but also at the Perdido Isle Historical Society Museum. Working at La Rinconada was a dream come true for the elderly matron, as well as for Gaspar, whose endless curiosity and inquisitiveness Miss Stewart's presence could only enhance.

Craig Cadawalader, Gaspar's new friend and sailing instructor, had signed on as captain of the *Floridablanca*, Uncle Charlie's one hundred and fifty foot Edwardian yacht. The yacht was currently under restoration from stem to stern in Naples, Florida and would soon be seaworthy and ready to sail by this coming summer. Between visits to the shipyard in Naples to assess the ship's progress, Craig kept busy teaching Gaspar and Alex how to sail.

The family's entire new-found fortune derived from a discovery made in the late 1800s by Gaspar's great uncle, Charles Munoz-Flores y Gaspar, who found the treasure of the legendary pirate Gasparilla. It was this mammoth haul which had been the source of all the riches at La Rinconada. In *The Mystery of the Gasparilla Succession*, Uncle Charlie's ghost personally instructed Gaspar as to the presence of treasure and how best he could go about finding it ... and find it he did. Gaspar had kept that discovery a secret from everyone, including his best friend Alex, vowing only to dip into it for personal reasons. But at fourteen years old, Gaspar had no idea what those "personal reasons" might be. What he did know was that he wanted the house and garden restored to their original glory and he definitely wanted to travel and see the world too. As the new laird of Perdido Isle, he also felt a duty to the people living there to somehow better their lives. This again was a thought, which he needed to develop further.

Gaspar was well aware that despite the riches he had found, his greatest discovery was Uncle Charlie ... or at least his ghost. The house was definitely haunted, in a really good way, by *good-time-Charlie* himself. Charlie had guided Gaspar through all the trials and tribulations, which had presented themselves since the kid's arrival just three months ago on Perdido Isle.

Peter Cawthorne was another important new friend. The lawyer, who'd discovered the Brown's right to the inheritance, had become invaluable to Gaspar and his mother. Peter was what Gaspar called *good goods*, and had become a most trusted advisor, friend and father figure. That Peter and Elvira should fall in love, was a dream come true for Gaspar, as his own father was deceased. For now the attractive couple were only engaged, but the wedding had been set for the summer. Gaspar secretly planned to take them on an amazing honeymoon, which would also be the maiden voyage of Uncle Charlie's restored yacht *Floridablanca*.

Life on Perdido Isle had not been dull since the Browns' arrival. He'd done battle with the board of directors of the Perdido Isle Historical Society Museum, who wanted to steal the land from him so that they could sell it to each other at low prices, before reselling it to others for a fortune. Also with the help of Alex and some of his other pals, he'd been able to assist the local police and coast guard in apprehending and arresting Unzega, the hated drug smuggler from the Yucatan. All in all, life since arriving on Perdido Isle had been full of adventure, discovery and growth for young Gaspar.

CHAPTER I

SCHOOL DAYS

S UMMER VACATION HAD SUDDENLY COME TO A SCREECH-ING HALT FOR GASPAR AND HIS PALS AS THE FIRST DAY of school would begin early the next morning. Sitting in his fanciful bedroom at La Rinconada, which had been built by Uncle Charlie to resemble the captain's cabin on a pirate's ship, he planned the coming days with his pal Alex.

"You're gonna like Jackson," Alex told him, referring to Andrew Jackson Junior High where both boys would be attending classes. "Besides Kevin, Pat, Sancho and Mark, you're gonna meet a lot of great guys and even a couple of girls who are pretty groovy too," Alex assured him.

"It's been such an amazing summer of adventure," Gaspar reminded his friend, thinking back on all they

1

had experienced these past three months. "I'm really looking forward to starting school, Al, and to making a lot of new friends too."

Early the next morning, Gaspar and Alex met in the motor court of La Rinconada, which was midway between the big house, where Gaspar lived with his mother, and the apartment over the stables, where Alex lived with his parents. Together the two boys marched down the crushed-shell driveway and out the gate to await the bus into town.

The ride to school took thirty minutes. Soon the boys were bounding up the stairs of Andrew Jackson Junior High School in Calaluna, one of the two towns on Perdido Isle. Together they found their homeroom and from there they learned the schedule of classes that they would be attending. A combination of math, English, American history, science and physical education had been mapped out for them. Auto Shop with Mr. Gunn was the class that both boys opted for as an extracurricular activity (although neither of them was old enough to drive).

Alex reveled in introducing "his new best friend" Gaspar, to all the kids in their class, while showing him around the extensive campus, which sprawled all the way down to the breaking waves of the Gulf of Mexico.

"Cool," was Gaspar's opinion of the playground, which was unfenced all the way to the water's edge. "Are we allowed to swim during recess, Al?"

"Yeah, a lot of kids go swimming or surfing, or just play on the sand. A lot of us like to play basketball, football, baseball and volleyball out here, too," Alex informed him.

Gaspar enjoyed his first day at school, meeting his teachers, and getting to know a new group of kids his own age. Because Gaspar had led his pals Alex, Kevin, Sancho, Pat and Mark in helping the police and the coast guard with the capture and imprisonment of the evil Mexican drug king, Unzega, Gaspar was considered a *star*, and was welcomed with open arms by his fellow students.

In all the excitement and camaraderie swirling around the first day of school, Gaspar noticed that there was one student who stood apart, *literally*. She was a thin girl, a little taller than him, which wasn't saying much since Gaspar only stood four feet, eleven inches tall. She wore a drab beige shift with faded gingham trim and a high-collared white blouse. Her most striking features were two long shiny black braids which she'd tied to each side of her head with bows made of red yarn. Her huge black, watery cow-like eyes seemed to be begging for compassion. Seeing that nobody was paying any attention to her, Gaspar stepped over to where she was watching from the sidelines and introduced himself.

"Hi, I'm Gaspar."

"I know," she answered shyly.

"What's your name?"

"My name's Iilona."

"That's an interesting name," Gaspar commented. "Is that an old family name?"

"It's my name. My family are Seminole. This was all our land before the Spanish came," she said, gesturing around her.

For some reason Gaspar felt a pang of guilt, but quickly shook it off, remembering that Uncle Charlie had paid cash for the entire 500,000 acres back in 1890. "Are you from the mainland?"

"No, like all my family, I was born on Perdido Isle. I live with my mother and my grandmother at the Seminole Spring. I'd like to show you our house, and introduce you to my family."

"If you were born on Perdido Isle, you must know all the kids here at school."

"I know who they are." She almost sounded apologetic.

"I only mention it because you seem ... alone." Gaspar winced as he said the dirty word.

"I am not alone," she said. "I just like to watch," she added weirdly.

"Okay," Gaspar said in his most understanding tone of voice. "It's been a pleasure talking with you, Iilona. I'll be seeing you around." He waved, turning back to where Alex and the gang were carousing, while wondering what the *drivelswiggers* Iilona was all about.

The first day of school went by in a flash. Before he knew it, days had turned into weeks and weeks into months, as Gaspar and Alex settled into a *school days* routine, which would certainly only vary with the seasons. He knew, or was known by, almost all the kids in his class and had made a good solid group of friends who he hung out with all the time. Iilona wasn't one of the gang, but he ran into her now and then. Or at least he saw her, here and there, and always stopped to chat with the loner. He felt it was his duty as a popular boy to go out of his way for her, especially since she seemed to be such an unpopular girl. He couldn't put his finger on it, but there was definitely something about Iilona that didn't quite meet the eye.

CHAPTER 2

EARNING THEIR WHEELS

WHEN NOT CAROUSING WITH THEIR PALS, GASPAR AND ALEX COULD BE FOUND USING THE SKILLS THAT MR. Gunn had taught them in auto shop, helping Lamar Washington fix up the old Ford woody, which had been abandoned in the stables. Gaspar had insisted on hiring Lamar, who was a driver at the Grand Hotel Floride in Llojeta, because as he explained to his mother, "I need wheels. "The old woody station wagon had been rotting in the stables for decades. Gaspar had his eye on that car from the first day he'd arrived at La Rinconada, when Alex had shown it to him. He couldn't wait for the old wagon to be in good enough condition to tool him and Alex and their pals around the island in style.

With Lamar working on the old car by day, and Gaspar and Alex helping him after school, it didn't take long before the team had the old rattle trap's V-8 purring like a tiger. Lamar had previously taken out the seats and sent them into town to be reupholstered in a deep green leather, which was the identical color of the original split and rotting leather they were replacing.

When Lamar pulled up to Andrew Jackson Junior High in the restored woody that Friday afternoon, Gaspar and Alex nearly fell over. All the kids gathered around to "ooh and aah" at the remarkable old Ford. Of course everyone wanted a ride, so Gaspar and Alex formed all the kids into a line and instructed Lamar to drive seven kids—three in the back, two in the front and two in the very back—up one side of Main Street and back down the other, before picking up another group of kids and then another for a similar once around the block.

When the line was down to the last five kids, Alex darted for the men's room. Waiting alone by the curb for the woody to return, Gaspar noticed Iilona standing off to the side under an elm tree. Sauntering over to her, he asked, "Iilona, don't you want to go for a whirl in the woody with the rest of the kids?"

"No, thank you, Gaspar," she trilled shyly. "I just like to watch. They all look like they're having such a good time. It's a lovely old car, Gaspar. Did you really restore it yourself?"

"Not all by myself," Gaspar corrected her. "Alex and I both helped, but Lamar did the bulk of the work, not us."

"What will you restore next, Gaspar?"

"Oh, I don't know. There's an old Riva motorboat in the stables. It would be a thrill to fix her up and take her out into the gulf. Do you like boats, Iilona?" Gaspar asked.

"Oh, no. My family and I, we don't like the water, not any more. Of course, there's water at the Seminole Spring, but we never go in it or on it, for that matter. We're just too scared."

"What are you scared of, Iilona? Perdido Isle is surrounded by water, I don't understand."

"You're new here, Gaspar. Wait until hurricane season. You'll understand then."

"Oh, well, I understand now. But according to the locals, there hasn't been a deadly bad storm hitting here since 1915 and I guess that one was a real doozy."

"Yes, that one was bad. But there have been others, not as severe, but still very scary, believe me." Iilona shuddered.

"Well, here comes the car, Iilona. May I drop you anywhere?" Gaspar inquired solicitously as Lamar brought the old woody to a halt in front of them.

"No, thank you. But I still want you to come to the Seminole Spring to see where I live."

"I'd like that, Iilona. But not today, maybe next week," Gaspar suggested.

"Goodbye, Gaspar."

"Goodbye, Iilona. See you next week," Gaspar hollered and waved, while jumping into the car next to Lamar as Alex flung himself into the back seat.

"Villa Gaspar, Lamar." Gaspar instructed. "Llojeta awaits."

CHAPTER 3

THE JEWEL HEIST

"WHAT'S THE NEWS, LAMAR?" GASPAR ASKED HIS DRIVER. "WHAT'S BEEN HAPPENING AROUND town while Alex and I've been stuck in school?"

"*Everyone's talk-in bout the big jewel heis at da hotel, Suh.*"

"JEWEL HEIST ... AT THE HOTEL," Gaspar shouted. "Are you kidding, Lamar?"

"*No, Suh, iz da truff. Some-un come in an stole some lady's jewls. Id-d happen t-day, roun bout one o'clock,*" Lamar drawled.

"Did the police catch the thieves, Lamar?" Alex hung on to the back of the old bench seat and stuck his head between Lamar and Gaspar.

"*No, suh. They dit git plum way, dis-speared inta thin air, they did!*"

"Where could they have gone? How many were there? Who was the victim, Lamar?" Gaspar pleaded.

"Donn no, suh. Guess yul hav-ta aks de pole-eece."

"It's a *rumfustian hornswaggle*," Gaspar proclaimed. "Jewel thieves on Perdido Isle! Al, we've got to get to the bottom of this. Lamar … head to Villa Gaspar by way of the Grande Hotel Floride!" Gaspar instructed.

When they got to the town of Llojeta at the eastern end of the island, they found themselves in the middle of a lot of commotion down by the hotel. Reaching the bottom of the street, Gaspar instructed Lamar to pull over to the curb so that he and Alex could jump out of the woody. Spying their pal, Sergeant O'Malley from the Calaluna Police Station, they ran up to him hoping for answers.

"Good afternoon, sergeant," Gaspar called, striding up to the heavy-set Irishman. "What's cook-in?"

"Hello, Gaspar. Hello, Alex," the sergeant greeted the boys happily. "There's been a big jewel heist this morning. A second floor job, big sparklers, a foreign lady, Señora Martinez de Gozz got tied up with her lady's maid, and robbed. No clues yet as to her attackers. Captain James from the local station here asked for reinforcements, so Captain Morgan sent me down to help out."

"Golly, Sarge, is this kind of thing a common occur-rence around here during the season?" Gaspar asked in earnest.

"Not a common occurrence, Gaspar. But not surprising, when you think of the rich folk that make Llojeta their winter stomping grounds. You can imagine how upset the hotel manager, Mr. Wilson is about this. This kind-a puts a black mark on the place, and a damper on all the grand festivities that the folks around here have been planning. I'm glad we don't have these kinds of problems in Calaluna, *knock on wood*," the sergeant chuckled, looking around for something other than his head to rap his knuckles against.

"Well, Sarge, as things transpire, please let me and Al know. You know how interested we are in everything that goes on around here," Gaspar begged.

"Of course, Gaspar, whatever we find out, you'll be the first to know. Why don't you drop by the precinct tomorrow and talk with Captain Morgan about it. I know he'll be happy to share any information he has with you."

"Thanks, Sarge," both boys called as they clamored back into the woody.

CHAPTER 4

THE VILLA GASPAR

GASPAR HAD PLANS TO TURN HIS OTHER HOUSE, *VILLA GASPAR*, LOCATED IN THE RESORT TOWN OF LLOJETA into a play house for his pals. Today he had Lamar drop him and Alex off there so they could plan how they wanted Uncle Charlie's old *facsimile Venetian palace* set up for fun. There was already a lavish billiard room with walls covered in dark green felt set off by dark mahogany moldings and fretwork. But what else they needed to make it an interesting place to hang out, was anyone's guess.

"Darts," Alex suggested, "we should have a dart board."

"And Monopoly, chess and checkers too," Gaspar added.

Yeah, and a bank of computers so we can play computer games, "Alex insisted.

17

"No, Al, no computer games!" Gaspar was insistent. "They're too isolating. We need interactive games that we can all play together, face-to-face, not just staring at a computer screen by ourselves."

"Well, that's a new one on me," Alex admitted, "but I get your message and it makes sense. No use in us all getting together if we're not going to talk and wrestle and have fun together." Alex agreed.

"You're reading me loud and clear, Al. Where do you think we should set all this up … in the living room or in the breakfast room?" Gaspar wondered out loud.

"Don't mess up the front rooms, Gasp … the breakfast room would work perfectly as a game room and the dining room could be used like a boardroom where we could have those round table discussions you're always talking about … *Wha-da-ya* say?"

"I agree completely … and the library should be a library. But we should re-stock it with books and comic books, cool videos and magazines for boys our age," Gaspar insisted.

"We'll need food and a media room." Alex never had food far from his mind.

"That's easy. We'll hire a caterer on the days that the club meets. And the old smoking room will make a great screening room." Gaspar breezed over that problem.

"What about the bedrooms?" Alex asked.

"Off limits," Gaspar made short shrift of that question. "Wha-da-we want with bedrooms, Al. We have several bathrooms down here, and those should be enough."

"Who's gonna join this club?" Alex asked.

"It's not a club, Al." Gaspar set him straight. "Whoever we want to goof off with will be invited. We'll only meet on Sundays, and we'll take it from there. Whoever we invite over to play will be able to bring one friend at a time with them. If we like that person we … you and I, can decide if we want them to be part of our gang." Gaspar laid down the law.

"Wow. Gasp. Everyone's gonna-wanna be invited."

"Yeah, and if we think they're like-minded … we'll invite them. Let's start slow, just us and our pals Kevin, Pat, Sancho, and Mark, and take it from there."

"How 'bout a soda fountain?" Alex was back on track.

"Great idea, we'll turn Uncle Charlie's pub room into a soda fountain. That'll be fun."

"What's your plan for the ballroom, Gasp?"

"*I-da-no, whaa-da-ya* think? Gaspar hadn't given it much thought. "We could put a basketball hoop at each end, and we could mess around with roller skates in there, and if we want to, we could even *dance*."

"*Dance*, are you kidding!"

"No, Al, I'm not."

"You're not dancing with me, *mister*." Alex responded in no uncertain terms.

"Don't mess with me, you *dissembling, dizzy-eyed codpiece*, or the only dance you'll be doin' will be the *Hempen Jig*, and believe me you won't be *doin' it* with me, *you reeky, plume-plucked-miscreant*. Of course I don't wanna dance with you. But we … you and me and the gang, should learn to dance, and dance well. Maybe I'll bring in a dance instructor, and someone who can teach us table manners too, like in the old movies. Yeah and maybe someone who has a lot of style should be invited to come over and teach us how to dress, not just for business, but to impress girls too.

"GIRLS!" Are we gonna be invitin' girls?" Alex was flabbergasted.

"We're not gonna be inviting girls, *you beslubbering, beef-witted barnacle*. But maybe we'll have a proper dinner dance once a month or maybe we'll want to dress up, like Fred Astaire or Cary Grant, and it's just possible we'd actually like it."

"And what if the guys don't?"

"Then they don't have to join us, Al. Anyway, inviting the girls is gonna be an individual situation. So, yes … *you* will be inviting a girl to be your date, and so will I and the other guys too," Gaspar informed him in no uncertain terms.

For some reason, Gaspar suddenly thought of Iilona and wondered how she would fit into his vision of a glamorous dinner dance in her beige shift and high-collared blouse and her long shiny braids. Try as he might, he couldn't shake the vision of Iilona standing there in the ballroom with her big cow eyes, looking drab in his glittering *turn of the century* interior.

"Wow!" Alex brought him out of his daydreams and exhaled. "This is *revolutionary*, Gasp! Wait till the guys hear your idea. Their reactions will be a testament to how popular you really are, *or aren't*."

"That's an interesting reaction, Al. I guess we're just gonna have to wait and see what happens. But it's *my* house and *my* invitation, and if they don't want to play by *my* rules, then it's not gonna affect me one way or the other." He rested his case.

"Gasp, that's why I like you. You live in your own world, and you live by your own rules."

"That's right, Al. *Damn the torpedoes, full speed ahead*! We'd better get home before we get in trouble for staying out too late. Lamar should be outside by now." Gaspar turned to go. Sure enough, by the time they'd closed up the place and stepped outside, Lamar was waiting for them in the driveway.

"Let's go to Karen's Café and grab a bite before heading home," Alex suggested.

"Good idea, Al. Lamar, let's all go to Karen's and get some chow." Gaspar insisted.

Before they knew it, the car was pulling up outside of Karen's Café. It was almost six o'clock and the two friends were ready for sustenance.

"Can we get you something, Lamar?" Gaspar asked the driver politely.

"No, suh. Thank-y vera much, I'va got suppah wait-in on me back home. Thank-y suh. Thank-y vera much." Lamar smiled broadly.

Striding into the coffee shop, the boys took two seats at the almost deserted counter where Karen greeted them with her special brand of indifferent affection.

"Gaspar, Alex, come on in and take the load off. What can I get you mates?" the boisterous waitress hollered from behind the counter.

"Well, Karen, I'm not really very hungry. So why don't you just bring me a *mousetrap* on a t*oasted English muffin*, and a *glass of baby juice*, and you can top it all off with a *Dusty Miller*." Gaspar hoped he'd gotten Karen's Café lingo down pat.

"Yeah, echoed Alex. I don't want to spoil my dinner, so I'll have the same."

"Wha-da-ya-mean, not spoil your dinner. This is your dinner," Gaspar interjected.

"I like to think of this as my *hors d'oeuvres*," Alex giggled at his attempt to speak French. "Tonight, my mom's making albondigas soup, chicken taquitos and a chile relleno casserole … all my favorite dishes," he smiled with expectation, smacking his lips.

"God's teeth, Al. *You yeasty, whey-faced scut*, and you're not *invitin'* me," Gaspar complained. *"Zounds, I ne'er thought thou wouldst do that to a poor miserable scains-mate*

like me!" Gaspar cajoled his friend in his own brand of *pirate speak.*

"Shut-up, Gasp, you *puny, puking maggot-pie*. You know you're always invited. My mom would much rather feed a *reeky, onion-eyed minnow* like you any day of the week than a *plume-plucked-miscreant* like me. All she ever talks about is how skinny and underweight you are. Her secret desire is to fatten you up like the wicked witch did to that *loggerheaded, half-faced hedge-pig* Hansel," Alex howled.

"Good one, Al. But you know that's ridiculous. To prove you wrong, I'm coming over tonight, uninvited … just to see what happens."

"Be my guest, you *wag-tailed scallywag*. See what I care," Alex challenged him.

"*Go to, Al, you dry fool. I'll no more of you: besides, you grow dishonest.* Anyone who could call me *puny* is a *tickle-brained* liar." Gaspar laughed as he joked about his own, tiny four foot eleven inch, ninety-pound frame.

Karen listened to the boys exchanging their pirate insults with exquisite disinterest. "Are you two *surly, rump-fed, puttocks* finished gabbing? Do ya want to eat here or would you prefer to go back to the *hacienda* and have your madre's enchiladas?" she said in her most bored drawl.

"Oh no, Karen. Give us the works right now! You know what we wanna hear," Gaspar enthused.

"Hey Frank," Karen yelled through the pass-through to her long-suffering short order cook, "*shake a leg*, it's *customer service time*. I need two *G.A.C.S* and *burn the British*! Fill two glasses with *moo juice*, and top it all off with a couple of *Dusty Millers*." She finished placing the boys order as only she knew how in her own inimitable *patois*.

"*Eighty-six the Dusty Millers*," Frank yelled back, without emotion.

"No *Dusty Millers*, boys. How 'bout *a couple o buckets of cold mud*, instead?" Karen asked them without showing the slightest interest in what their answer might be.

"No *Dusty Millers!*" Gaspar had set his heart on a serving of Frank's fabulous chocolate pudding, sprinkled with powdered malt.

"I don't want a *bucket of cold mud*, Karen. Plain old chocolate ice cream just doesn't do it for me today," Alex interjected.

"Tell you what," Gaspar brightened. "Bring us a couple of *double black cows* instead and *eighty six* the *sweet Alice*," he said, canceling the order for the two glasses of milk.

"Do ya want some *tommy* on that *G.A.C.*?" Karen pronounced it *jack*, even though Gaspar and Alex knew it stood for *grilled American cheese*.

"Naw, Karen. You know we're *anti-vegetarian*," Gaspar quipped.

"Tomatoes supposed to be a fruit," Karen informed him.

"Even worse," Alex joked.

"I read somewhere that knowledge is knowing that a tomato is a fruit … but wisdom is knowing not to put it in a fruit salad," Gaspar quipped.

"Ha, ha, very clever," Karen responded, nonplussed. "So now you're going to talk to me in *paraprosdokians*. Let's get down to business boys, what's goin' on?" Karen asked. "What's the news out there and how are they *treatin'* you guys at school?"

"School's great. I've met so many new friends," Gaspar beamed. "Have you ever heard of the Seminole Spring*?*"

"No, what's that? Some fancy new kind of mineral water?" Karen scratched her scalp with her pencil.

"No, it's a place. My friend Iilona lives there. She wants me to go there with her and check it out."

"Never heard of it," Karen snapped.

"Did you hear about the robbery in Llojeta?" Alex changed the subject.

"It's all people will talk about," Karen complained. "All *I* want to talk about are *people* and all they want to talk about are *rubies, diamonds and emeralds.* I don't see what all the fuss is about. The junk was insured, no doubt, and if it wasn't, the old woman can always buy more. You can bet there's plenty more *South American scudi* where that came from." Karen assured them dismissively.

Karen turned towards the pass-through, announcing as she turned back around … "Here's your tea party, boys.

Let me know if you want anything else," she pronounced placing their orders in front of them.

"Thanks, Karen. What a feast. Do you think I should have asked Frank to *burn some bacon* to go on the *G.A.C.*?"

"It's not too late. Everything tastes better with bacon, *even chocolate cake*." Karen wasn't joking. "Frank, *burn some bacon, on the fly*," she shouted to the short-order cook. "We're making a *Jack Benny* here."

"Tell them to hold their horses," Frank yelled back.

"They need it on the fly," Karen reproached him.

"If they want it any faster, tell em' to go to *Swifties*," Frank cracked, referring to the soda fountain in Llojeta.

Gaspar and Alex looked at each other knowingly, with huge smiles spread across their faces. Hearing Karen and Frank quarrel was one of the main reasons for sitting at the counter.

"What's a Jack Benny?" Alex hadn't heard that one.

"Ham and cheese, kid. It's named after that old *ham* … Jack Benny."

"Jack Benny is one of my favorite comedians, Karen. His best film was *The Broadway Melody of 1936*. Did you ever see that one?" Gaspar chimed in.

"No, Gaspar. Black and white films turn me off," Karen confessed, "and musicals make me itch."

"Oh, Karen, you haven't lived till you've seen all the Broadway Melodies. One has a professional sneezer and another has a professional snorer. They're amazing movies, and *The Broadway Melody of 1940* even has Fred Astaire," Gaspar enthused.

Karen and Alex weren't as impressed by old movies or old movie stars as Gaspar was. Instead, while pretending to listen to him expound on the glories of the old films, Alex concentrated on his sandwich, while Karen spent her time looking out the window while scratching her arm while simultaneously watching the action inside the café.

"*Check out the ice*, and get a load of the *codfish* with her," Karen interrupted Gaspar's solo review of the Broadway Melody. She shrugged toward a pair of good-looking newcomers, who'd just taken *a seat in the gallery.*

Gaspar discreetly turned around to check out the pretty girl who'd just come in and the flashy dude with her. They'd taken a booth by the window, and had started perusing the menu.

"Have you ever seen them before, Karen?" Gaspar wanted to know.

The big-hearted *soup jockey* just shook her head in the negative and whispered "I've never seen anything even remotely like them before."

"Maybe they're new in town," Gaspar suggested, taking a bite of his sandwich.

"Something tells me they're just passing through. I'll find out while you finish your *J.B.* You sure you don't want Frank to put some *love apples* on that?"

"No, Karen, whether fruit or legume, I don't want any tomatoes." Gaspar insisted while Alex, mouth full, shook his head in agreement.

Karen just shrugged her shoulders indifferently as she walked around the counter to where the walk-in's were sitting. Heading straight for their booth, Karen gave the newcomers the once over and her own version of the third degree. It didn't take her long to discover that they'd been staying the week at the Grand Hotel Floride in Llojeta and had come to Calaluna to visit the museum and see the town before going back to the hotel for the night.

"Just passing through," she reported to Gaspar and Alex after yelling at Frank to "*Walk two cows through the garden, cremate them and make them cry*" and "while you're at it, Frank, *draw two in the dark flowing Mississippi.*"

Gaspar loved Frank's burgers with everything on them, especially raw onion, but he feared he'd never learn to like coffee … not even with cream and sugar. "Who are they?" he inquired.

"A couple of swells, staying at the Grand Hotel Floride. I guess they decided to go slumming this afternoon. He's a foreign fellow with a thick Teutonic accent … looks like a dude … probably a gambler, and she must be his moll," Karen said, not mincing words. Something tells me they've come to Perdido Isle looking for adventure.

While Karen paid attention to her other customers, Gaspar phoned Lamar and arranged for him and Al to be picked up out in front of the café. He didn't know what Karen had told the newcomers, but they seemed mighty interested in the two boys sitting at the counter. He knew that Karen's idea of a secret, like Oscar Wilde's, was *to tell only one person at a time*. He could just imagine what she might have told the strangers about her best friend, the boy billionaire. It was one of the liabilities of liking Karen so much. She had a heart of gold, but her gossip made Radio Free Europe seem deaf and dumb.

CHAPTER 5

A GANG OF TWELVE

GASPAR AND ALEX PROCEEDED WITH THEIR PLANS FOR THE SOCIAL CLUB AND IN NO TIME AT ALL HAD everything in place, ready to extend invitations to their pals kevin, Pat, Sancho and Mark.

"Al, how 'bout a core group of twelve friends instead of just the six of us to get this going. I think twelve is a better number for starting this out? *Wha-da-ya think*? Gaspar asked.

"Not a bad idea," Alex responded. "Besides the six of us, *how-bout invitin'* Jimmy Townsend, Frank Cassidy, and Tommy Sullivan too?"

"Yeah, and I was thinking of Tim Scanlan, George White and Travis Bryant." Gaspar threw his names into the ring.

"Let's do it."

31

"Okay. Tomorrow I'll ask those twelve *swag-bellied skains-mates* to join us and that's all. They're not invited to bring guests, not this first time. We'll meet on Sunday, and you and I will make all the arrangements."

The following Sunday, twelve boys wearing jeans and t-shirts, cutoffs and sneakers, made there way by bus and bike to Villa Gaspar in Llojeta. When they got there, Gaspar opened the door personally and led them into the extravagantly decorated ruby brocade and crimson velvet-lined living room with its white and gold-painted paneling. The initial reaction to the extremely rich but dated décor was silence except for George White who, as an admitted devotee of old movies on TCM, made it clear that he loved the theatricality of it all.

"This is the most aggressively opulent room I've ever seen," George proclaimed upon entering the magnificent salon, "and I mean … even in the movies!"

When all of the charter members of his club had assembled, Gaspar told them why they were there.

"Welcome, mates. Let me tell you why I've invited you here today. This is my house. It's part of my inheritance from my Uncle Charlie. This is the way it was decorated when I got it, and I'm not planning to change it. Al and I thought it would be fun to turn this into a playhouse for us and our pals. In a minute I'll give you a tour of the place. What I want to do is invite you to come here every Sunday, like a club. You are each invited to bring one friend with you and if we like him … we means

Al and me, we'll invite him to come back. By the way, I mean *him*. This is a *gentlemen's* group, so no girls please.

All the boys, *um hmmmed* in unison, shaking their heads up and down in agreement.

"This lady is Mrs. Hobart," Gaspar said, introducing an older woman who had just entered the room. He watched as seven boys stood up, nodding and smiling towards Mrs. Hobart. "Stand up when a *lady* enters the room!" Gaspar commanded the five still-seated dolts who immediately sprang to attention.

"Pleased to meet you, ma'am," was mumbled out of ten uncomfortable mouths.

"Please be seated, gentlemen," Mrs. Hobart begged.

"Mrs. Hobart will be our house mother. If you need anything while you're here, just ask Mrs. Hobart and if it's within her power, she will get it for you," he advised, still scowling at the five doltish miscreants.

"Anything?" Mark asked.

"Anything within reason, Mark. As a gentleman, I know you would never want to take advantage of your host's hospitality," Gaspar assured him.

"Al and I have included a lot of things here that we think you'll like. That is a suggestion box," Gaspar said, pointing to a brass-studded mahogany box on the side table. "If you come up with any ideas you think would work, just put them in writing, in there."

"What do you call this room?" Travis asked innocently.

"We are sitting in the drawing room, or living room, if you will. We will use this room to hang out in. Come along, Al and I will show you around," Gaspar commanded. "Al, you lead the way."

"This is the dining room," Alex announced, leading the group into the large mahogany- paneled room across the hall. "We'll use this room for roundtable discussions."

"Wha-da-ya-mean?" Sancho sang out.

"Sancho, a roundtable discussion is one where we will all toss around a subject for discussion and listen to each other's opinions, without passing judgment. In other words, we will respect the personal opinions of others while aggressively getting our own points of view across," Gaspar explained.

"We'll also use the dining room for Sunday night dinners as well," Alex threw in.

"And I may also invite important men and women of letters to talk to us about current events, world affairs and subjects of artistic, scientific and educational value," Gaspar expounded.

"Sounds like school," Tim said scornfully.

"Unlike school, Tim, attending these special evenings or seminars is not mandatory. But I can guarantee you, if you don't attend you'll feel like a *warped, tickle-brained varlot* on Monday mornings when all your pals are discussing issues of importance with confidence and you're unable to participate without looking like a *clouted, clapper-clawed clay-brain*," Gaspar hit home without resistance.

"*A what*?" Tim insisted.

"Precisely, Tim, I rest my case," Gaspar guffawed and all the others joined in.

"The next room is the library," Alex cut in, hoping to change the subject, while leading the group into the magnificent book-lined room. "We've stocked the shelves with the best books for guys our age, with subjects like geography, science, world history, and look … all the best comic books and really cool videos and the latest magazines that we all like too."

"Consider this library your own," Gaspar stepped in. "You're welcome to check out any books or magazines on the shelves using the honor system. That means if you check it out … you have to bring it back … and if you don't … you might not be invited back when Sunday rolls around again. Mrs. Hobart will be keeping track of all the comings and goings here, so don't take her presence for granted. Isn't that right, Mrs. Hobart?" Gaspar asked his new house mother, who nodded her ascent.

"We have a media room right across the hall and a billiard room right over here at the end. We're planning to have a billiard tournament too, so you'll want to brush up on your game if you want to win a trophy." Alex alerted them, showing them the magnificent room which stretched the entire width of the house.

Moving to the former breakfast room, Gaspar announced, "This is the game room. As you can see we have six tables set up for Monopoly, chess, checkers and cards. One thing I want to make very clear is that we'll have no gambling in this house. I don't need any excuses for your parents not allowing you to come back. So guys, whatever you do, don't break the rules here. On that note, we'll have no smoking of any kind or consumption of alcohol either. And believe me, Mrs. Hobart is a former policewoman," Gaspar lied, "and is here to make sure that these rules are followed to a tee," he said, turning with a nod to Mrs. Hobart.

"We have a swimming pool out back," Gaspar said, leading the group out through the open French doors. "And a gym has been set up in the pool house. There are showers and changing rooms, as well as a dry sauna and a steam room, "he said, stepping into the gym and showing them the doors left and right leading to the two bathrooms and changing rooms. That's why I asked you to bring your trunks and gym clothes today. If you want to leave them here, we have lockers set up in the house too. Swimming is at your own risk guys, so take it easy out here and use common sense. I'm counting on you to exercise a lot of personal responsibility, which as you know, is a quality I pride myself on."

Heading back into the house, Alex said, "There's a cool, self-serve soda fountain set up in the old pub room. And we've put a dart board in there too." He showed them the room and pointed out his special contribution to the décor with pride.

"Gaspar, this is quite a set-up you've planned for us. It looks like Sundays are going to be full of fun and mind-blowing stimulation, too. What else have you got up your sleeve for us, Captain?" Kevin implored, using the nickname he always called Gaspar, from his seat on one of the bar stools at the soda fountain.

"Well, if we wanted to, we could turn ourselves into our own scout troop, and this house could be our headquarters. I also think of us as a social club and that means parties. And by parties, I mean boys and girls, dressed up and behaving like ladies and gentlemen. Since I know all *you goatish, gore-bellied guys* fairly well, I can say without fear of contradiction that all of us, including myself, could use some polishing up in the *gentleman* category. Therefore, I want to bring in someone to teach us how to dance … all kinds of dancing. And someone who can teach us how to dress sharp, like Cary Grant, and someone who will teach us how to behave like gents at the dining table … what forks and spoons to use, and to teach us what is expected of us as perfect guests too.

"Sounds kinda sissy, Gasp," Tommy spoke up.

"No, Tommy. It's not *sissy*, or *girlie*. It's *manly* to behave properly, to dress with style, to cultivate taste and connoisseurship, and to have good manners. It will set us up to be accepted everywhere, as men of the world. Believe me, this is not the main thrust of what I want to do here. But it will play a great role in our growing up, and going out into the world to colleges and businesses outside the confines of tiny little Perdido Isle. There's a big world out there guys, and we've gotta be prepared to take it over.

"Gasp, tell them the good part!" Alex urged, thinking Gaspar might be losing his audience again.

"Come with me," Gaspar said, saving the best for last, he led them into the villa's amazing, mirrored and crystal chandelier-hung ballroom.

When he pushed open the massive double doors leading into the double height space the other boys let out a collective, *ohh myyy gawdd*!

Without missing a beat or taking any notice of his friends' discomfort or collective awe, Gaspar stated his plan. "My thought is that we have a proper dinner dance here in the ballroom once a month. That is, after we all learn how to behave properly. In the meantime, I thought we could put up a couple of removable basketball hoops at either end so we can skirmish.

"I think I'd like that better than dancing," Pat enthused.

"Pat, tell me that after you have a couple of lessons, gain a little self confidence and hold a girl in your arms at your first dance," Gaspar challenged his pal.

"I don't think I'll ever be any good at dancing," Pat mumbled inaudibly.

"Anyway, let's not all get excited. I've invited you here to have fun, so as long as we're here, how 'bout some lunch?"

With that, Gaspar lead the group into the kitchen where Mrs. Hobart had set up a buffet of sandwiches and cold drinks.

"Lunch is self-serve, gentlemen," Mrs. Hobart told them in her most ladylike way. Help yourselves, please. I've set up a table outside on the terrace for you.

Bringing their heaping plates to the long table that Mrs. Hobart had set for twelve, they all started talking at once, exchanging ideas and enthusing about how much fun Sundays were going to be from now on. Before lunch was over, Kevin had challenged Gaspar to a game of chess. Pat had vowed to thump Sancho at checkers, and Alex, Mark, Tommy and Tim had already chosen their tokens for a competitive game of Monopoly. Jimmy and Frank said they'd head to the library to check out the videos and some of the new comic books that Gaspar had assembled there.

"Can we watch a video, Gasp?" Jimmy asked.

"Consider the house yours, guys, and treat it with care and respect, like it's your own. The video equipment is easy. If you guys can't figure it out or have any trouble, just ask Mrs. Hobart to help you. And listen, guys, while you're here, if you see anything wrong, anything out of place, anything missing, broken or out of order, please tell Mrs. Hobart. She is here to help keep everything in good repair. Don't be afraid to speak up. She is a friend first, and our housemother second.

Mrs. Hobart brought out a freshly baked berry pie and a bowl of vanilla ice cream, which she served to the happy friends who'd taken to her as if she might be their grandmother or great aunt.

The rest of the afternoon was dedicated to games, swimming, old movies and a delicious dinner, which Mrs. Hobart served on trays in the media room, while the boys watched Orson Wells in *Citizen Kane*.

When 9:30 rolled around, Gaspar shooed his pals out the door. "In the future," he told them, "9:30 will always be the official closing time for the clubhouse, so as not to upset any of our parents." He also told them, "Next time you come, I want to meet all of your parents, so that they can see this place and meet Mrs. Hobart, too. I want to assure them that they are welcome to visit the house while we're here having fun, any time."

After everyone had cut out, Gaspar thanked Mrs. Hobart and bid her goodnight.

CHAPTER 6

UNCLE CHARLIE APPROVES

LAMAR WAS IN THE WOODY, WAITING OUT IN FRONT. GASPAR AND ALEX JUMPED INTO THE PURRING CAR AND without a word, sped off in the direction of La Rinconada.

"See you at eight thirty, Lamar," Gaspar reminded him as the car rolled to a stop.

"*I'll be heah bright an oily to get you young gentlemen to school. Good-nigh,*" Lamar called, before driving off.

"I'll see you in the morning, Gasp." Alex bid good night, as he headed for his parents' apartment over the stables.

"Yeah," Gaspar called back. "like Lamar said, eight thirty. We don't *wanna* be late for homeroom again, Al." With that final reminder, he stepped through the big, wrought iron and glass front door of La Rinconada, and closed it quietly behind him.

43

Before leaving the house that day, Gaspar had told his mother not to wait up for him, that he was going to Villa Gaspar and that he would be back by ten. Entering the big hall, he could see that the rest of the house was dark, so he scurried upstairs, past his mother's closed bedroom door. He could hear her moving around inside, but decided not to bother her and went directly to the captain's cabin, which was his bedroom. As he'd hoped Uncle Charlie, or rather his ghost, was waiting for him, dressed impeccably and incongruously for a big game safari complete with khaki pants, jacket and pith helmet.

"Gasp, I thought you'd never get here," Charlie fretted.

"What's your rush, Uncle Charlie?" Gaspar asked.

"I'm late for a hunt in Mombasa. I've got a date with a Danish baroness and a great white hunter, Charlie bragged. I learned long ago it's never a good idea to keep friends with loaded rifles waiting, even if they are ghosts."

"Well what are you doing sitting around here? You better get going," Gaspar suggested.

"But I want to talk to you about the boys' club, or whatever you're calling your group," Charlie explained.

"Were you there, uncle … for the meeting?" Gaspar gulped.

"Of course, I was. You can't keep me out of my own house, can you?"

"Well, technically, it's *my* house now, uncle, but definitely want *you* to be a charter member of the club. No question!"

"I knew you would," Charlie said. "All the best clubs all over the world always asked me to join first. They knew that they could always count on me as a charter member, to give them *élan*," he patted himself on the back.

"That's what we need in this new club, uncle, style and class. I wish I could get you to teach the guys how to dress. Look at you, all dressed up and late for the party."

"Don't remind me, Gasp. How many times have I told you, punctuality is the courtesy of kings. I've got to get going, but not before I tell you that I think what you're doing for your friends is to be commended. You'll probably get in a lot of trouble because of it, but I want you to know that at least I approve. By the way, have you heard anything new about the robbery at the hotel?" he asked full of excitement. "You know, Gasp, October is the start of the season in Llojeta … when all the swells come in on their yachts, open their big houses, take suites at the hotel and start giving parties at home. Or if they don't have a home, in the fancy restaurants. Just walk down Grand Avenue and take a look around … Llojeta has come alive. It's not like during the summer when the streets resembled a ghost town … now that's a subject I really know about," the old ghost chuckled. "The jewelers are open now and the clothing boutiques too, and the antique stores and art galleries are all bustling

45

with shoppers. Overnight Llojeta has become a booming resort, and apparently this year is so glamorous that our little bit of paradise has even attracted jewel thieves too."

"Has this ever happened before, uncle?" Gaspar asked anxiously.

"Oh, yes, a couple of times, actually. I'll never forget the time when Marie of Romania was in town, back in the 20s. I gave a big party for her at La Rinconada. Something similar happened then. And again in the 40s, when the duke and duchess came calling. That robbery happened in a private house, too. But this most recent crime was in one of the big hotel suites. They tied the lady up and took all her pretty baubles. She claims they were worth eight million."

"Eight million … *dollars*?" Gaspar gulped.

"Well, she *is* South American. Maybe she meant eight million *Bolivianos* or *soles* … I don't know, Gasp, but we can find out. Is anyone talking about the jeweled dagger?" Uncle Charlie questioned.

"A jeweled dagger?" Gaspar repeated. "Is that what was stolen?

"Amongst other jeweled treasures in the lady's possession," sniffed Uncle Charlie.

"I hadn't heard that a jeweled dagger had been taken. That sounds like something rare and valuable. You're sure it's a fact and not someone's idea of a romantic joke? You know how hearsay is, uncle," Gaspar said, confused by the lack of clarity in the *scuttlebutt*.

"I can't remember who I heard talking about a jeweled dagger." Uncle Charlie looked puzzled. "But I do know that a jeweled dagger has gone missing. I heard the lady bemoaning the fact to someone. She said it had come from Montegufoni, you know the Sitwell's medieval rock pile in the Pyrenees. Wonderful place, so romantic, oh the times we had there. Me and Edith, and dear Sacheverell and Reresby. Thrilling, simply thrilling. You know their father was mad as a hatter. He would only have white cows on the property and he had them all stenciled in blue ink with floral designs to make them look like they were made of blue and white Delft porcelain. *Delft cows*! Don't think I didn't want to copy that idea right here at La Rinconada, but then again ... who wants cows in the tropics? Anyway, you should have seen the lake, Gaspar. The decorative lake at Montegufoni. I was staying there the day that old Lord Sitwell woke up and decided on a whim that he'd have the lake moved from one side of the castle to the other. It was insanity,.. pure insanity, but so much fun to watch. Old Lord Sitwell was a wonderful host. He taught me everything I know about entertaining, Oh yes he did," Uncle Charlie enthused. "You know, Gasp, the castle was taken over by the dirty Nazis. But when the Sitwells got the place back, everything was still there, everything *but* the jeweled dagger on Sir Osbert's bedside table. I wonder, maybe there's more to that missing bejeweled *objet* than meets the eye." Uncle Charlie mused.

Gaspar didn't know what to make of Uncle Charlie's mental meanderings but stored the information for now, until he could digest it. *Lord Sitwell*, *Montegufoni*, I'll have to Google those for sure, he told himself.

"Anyway, these thieves apparently were cool customers and got away scot-free." Uncle Charlie was back on his soap box. "The police think they're the same gang who've been pulling similar stunts all along the Gulf from St. Petersburg to Naples, and now Perdido Isle. If they keep on their trajectory, Pensacola and New Orleans will be their next logical targets."

"A crime wave," Gaspar exhaled. "That's a lot to digest for one night, uncle. I better go back downstairs and lock the front door."

"Not a bad idea, Gasp, and I'd better hightail it to Mombasa before the natives on the dark continent get restless."

"Before you cut out, what did you mean by *trouble*, when I was telling you about my social club, uncle?" Gaspar questioned.

"Oh nothing, Gasp," Uncle Charlie smiled wickedly. "Just remember, *no good deed goes unpunished*!" The old ghost said, as he dashed through the wall to meet his friends in Mombasa.

After Uncle Charlie left, Gaspar headed downstairs to lock the door. He reached the bottom of the staircase just as his mother and Peter Cawthorne walked in.

"Mom, are you just getting home?" Gaspar asked confused.

"Yes, dear. Peter and I went to a movie in town. Did you and your friends have a fun day?"

"Yeah, we had a blast. But mom, I got home a half hour ago and I thought I heard you rummaging around in your room."

"No, darling. As you can see, Peter and I are just arriving. I promised him a cup of coffee and some ice cream. Would you like to join us in the kitchen? I've got your favorite chocolate fudge?"

"Mom, I'm telling you. There's someone in your room. Come on, Peter. I think we've got an intruder," Gaspar hollered as he ran back up the stairs, with Peter bounding right behind him.

Reaching the doors to the master bedroom at the same time, Peter threw them open and rushed into Elvira's room with Gaspar at his side. Together they stopped short at what they saw there.

"My room!" whaled Elvira, who stepped in behind them. "It's been ransacked," she cried, scared, confused and angry.

"Mom, I think you've been robbed," Gaspar said, running to the open French doors leading to the long balcony overlooking the Gulf of Mexico. Running outside he hung over the balustrade to see if anyone was running away. Just then he heard a powerful motor near the beach and could barely see a sleek speedboat taking off through the waves. "Peter, look, they're getting away." The sound of the roaring motor and Gaspar's cry brought Ramon, the night watchman, running. "Ramon, we've been burgled," Gaspar yelled down to the confused man, before disappearing back into the house. "Mom, look around. See if anything's missing, your jewels!" Gaspar ordered.

"Jewels, really Gaspar, don't be so theatrical. I haven't any jewels worth stealing, and I haven't any cash in the house. In fact I have nothing worth hiding or locking up. They were obviously looking for something valuable here," Elvira explained. "I can assure you, I had nothing here that a burglar would find of interest."

Gaspar loved his mom but had realized shortly after moving into La Rinconada that she didn't know, let alone care, that they were basically living in a museum, surrounded by valuable works of art and irreplaceable treasure. "Oh, mom, please, just look around. Look in your dressing room. Where do you keep your jewelry?" Gaspar implored her.

"Well, I keep my costume jewelry right here in the top drawer," Elvira explained, walking into her dressing room, in an attempt to placate her son. "Oh my goodness, look at the mess in here. They certainly left no stone unturned," she chuckled shaking her head. "Well, I'll be." she declared, "Would you look at that. They did take my costume jewelry. They must not be very bright if they think that old junk is worth stealing," she giggled shrugging her shoulders at Gaspar and Peter. "Well, boys, why don't you go downstairs and help yourselves to some ice cream and make a pot of coffee. I'll be down in a minute after I straighten this place up a little." Elvira shooed them out of her room, laughing.

When they got to the kitchen, Gaspar told Peter the truth. "Peter, there's something you need to know. My mother is adorable, but she hasn't got a clue. You know and I know that this house is full of treasure. The tiniest porcelain shepherdess is most probably a museum piece. She has no idea what she's surrounded with here. To her it's all just old furniture and bric-a-brac. Some of those jewels that are missing *were* costume jewelry, base metal and glass. But a lot of them were the real thing, part of cousin Eugenia Floride's collection. The old girl had it stashed here and there, all over the house. You know that I found a lot of it because you've sold it to pay for the yacht restoration. But I also gave some to mom, because I wanted her to have something genuine and valuable. I never told her it was valuable because she wouldn't have believed me. And if she had, she would have been too scared to wear it. So I just pretended that it was no big deal. Peter, I gave her a citrine and diamond parure. You know … a set … necklace, bracelet, earrings, ring and a great big floral brooch. It was all set in 18k gold-backed silver. Antique, like all of cousin Eugenia's stuff. There was a three-strand oriental pearl necklace, ten to sixteen millimeters, and another opera length strand of amazing fourteen millimeter pearls too. Do you remember them? There are framed photos downstairs of cousin Eugenia wearing them. Anyway, I gave my mother several sets ... an amethyst and diamond set, and an emerald one too. There was also a sapphire set and a lot of big rings as well. I've got photographs of all of it. I suppose I should have told her they were valuable, but you know how it is with women. I just didn't want a fuss," Gaspar finished off.

"I'll have to report this to Captain Morgan," Peter said, picking up the telephone. "Gaspar, go back upstairs and stop your mom from disturbing the crime scene. Just tell her to come down here until the cops arrive. Hurry," Peter instructed him.

Before the coffee had finished brewing, the house was swarming with cops, all of them intent on finding fingerprints and clues. Peter had asked them to come silently, without sirens blaring or flashing lights, so as not to disturb the Mendoza family. Sergeant O'Malley took down a detailed report and Gaspar promised to send an itemized list of the stolen *costume jewelry* along with photographs, to the police station in the morning. Peter had briefed the sergeant over the telephone that Mrs. Brown was unaware that the jewels, which had been part of the inheritance from her cousin Eugenia, were genuine. Peter had also told the sergeant that it would just muddy the waters and make things too dramatic around the house, if she were to discover now that her loss was significant. Because Gaspar was the actual heir

52

and the jewels had been his gifts to his mother, Peter told the sergeant that the request had come from Gaspar directly. He also told him that Gaspar, as well as he, would appreciate the policeman's discretion in the matter and that no press coverage of the break-in, was exactly what they all wanted.

CHAPTER 7

NEW DEVELOPMENTS

GASPAR HAD NEGLECTED TO TELL THE CHARTER MEMBERS OF THE CLUB TO KEEP HIS ELABORATE plans to themselves. By early Monday morning news of the group, along with updates about the big jewel robbery at the Grand Hotel Floride had spread like wildfire across the campus of the junior high. Wherever Gaspar turned, boys and girls stopped talking about the robbery of the South American lady, to ask him if they could join his club. The only answer he could come up with was that he didn't know what they were talking about. Quickly he rallied Alex and Kevin and sent them out across the playground to search for the others, and tell them if anyone asked them about the club that they were to answer the same … I don't know what you're talking about.

It was a disaster. Sitting down on a bench at the edge of the playground, he didn't notice that Iilona was sitting there also. Looking to his left, he was startled to see her, sitting very erect with her head turned towards him and her big watery cow eyes staring at him as if she wanted to plead with him over something. She was wearing the same beige shift with the funny gingham trim and the high-collared blouse with ruffles that she always wore. Her two braided pigtails were shiny black and as usual tied with bows made of red-colored yarn. Gaspar could have sworn the bench had been vacant before he'd sat down.

"Oh hello, Iilona," Gaspar greeted the awkward girl.

"Hello, Gaspar. Are you in trouble?" Iilona asked.

"Oh, I'm always in trouble," he chuckled. "What about you? What's up."

"Up? Oh, up, yes, well. I was just sitting here waiting for you, hoping you'd come out to the playground and sit down," Iilona said oddly.

"Iilona, wha-da-ya-mean, you were waiting for me? What if I didn't come out?"

"Oh, then I would have found you," she answered weirdly. "Have you heard anything new about the robbery at the Grand Hotel Floride? Anything about the jeweled dagger?"

"The jeweled dagger, what do you know about a jeweled dagger?"

"That's the most important piece that was stolen," Iilona informed him, matter-of-factly. "The key to the entire affair."

"Huh?"

"The robbery, it's all anyone's talking about."

Gaspar couldn't believe how awkward Iilona was in conversation. "Who told you about a jeweled dagger? What do you know about it that I don't know?" he asked the shy girl. "What do you mean, the key to the entire affair, what exactly does that mean Iilona?"

"Well, it was done by five men, wearing colorful sports clothes, you know like fancy golf clothes. They drove up to the service entrance of the hotel in a late model royal blue sedan. One of the men stayed behind the wheel with the engine running and turned the car around so the front faced the driveway out. The other four men entered the hotel, The Grande Hotel Floride, through the service entrance and took the service elevator up to the tenth floor and went directly to the Ambassador Suite. That's number 1025, the big two-bedroom suite facing the gulf with two terraces ... one on the north side and the other on the south side. They entered the suite using a pass key and surprised Señora Martinez de Gozz, tied her up with her own Hermes silk scarf, and gagged her with a pretty pink handkerchief with lace insets embroidered with her initials. Without the slightest difficulty, they opened her safe by dialing 25 right, 38 left and 93 right. They helped themselves to all of her sparklers, including a pendant diamond that she told the police was the first cutting of the *Koh-i-noor*," Iilona finished up matter-of-factly, without ever blinking an eye.

Gaspar, on the other hand, was exhausted by her diatribe and asked, "Iilona, how do you know all those details? Are you making them up?"

Iilona opened her eyes even wider than usual and said, "Oh, no, I got it first hand. They also tied up her lady's maid … used the strings from her apron to do it and gagged her with one of her own white cotton gloves. The poor girl was very upset. French you know … not accustomed to so much excitement."

"From who?" Gaspar asked again, hoping to get a straight answer.

"Oh, from a friend. From a very *good* friend," Iilona said quietly. "The funny thing is that the four men who came in through the service entrance were not the same four men who went out. They were wearing the same style clothes and hats, but they weren't the same men," Iilona giggled to herself nonsensically.

"Huh," Gaspar liked her, but really thought she was a strange one. "What else is it, Iilona? Why were you waiting for me here? Surely not to tell me that crazy story about the jewel robbery at the hotel and a mysterious jeweled dagger. What's really on your mind?" Gaspar asked her. "Do you want to be a member of my non-existent club too?"

"Oh. no. I don't know about that. I was just thinking about you, and hoping you could help me."

"In what way? Just get to the point, Iilona." Gaspar didn't want to be rude, but the girl's manner was really exasperating.

"Well, I thought maybe, some day after school, you'd come to *the Seminole Spring* and visit me and my mother and grandmother. They would like very much to meet you."

"Oh, is that all," Gaspar breathed a little easier. "You asked me over the first time I met you, on my first day of school. I think I told you then that I'd love to see where you live. As for your grandmother and mother, I'd love to meet them too. Why don't you bring them to La Rinconada for tea or something, and I could introduce all of you to *my* mother as well."

"No, no," Iilona stuttered and hesitated. "No, I'd like you to come to *our* house ... *alone*," she added mysteriously.

"Oh, golly ... well, okay. Where do you live again?" Gaspar just wanted to get out of there.

"We live at the Seminole Spring," she said cryptically. "When can we expect you?"

"Oh, well, Iilona, I've got a lot going on right now, but I'll let you know. Maybe, I can visit you next week or the week after that. I've some big plans for this weekend, but next week ... or the week after ... I promise," he said, standing up and waving, while extricating himself from the sticky situation. "See you later, Iilona. See you soon, I promise," he said, breaking into a run for his next class as the school bell sounded in the distance. He hoped that he hadn't been too rude to the awkward girl. Gaspar couldn't bear it if he thought he'd hurt someone's feelings. He knew that Iilona and her hurt feelings, which he was now imagining, would be on his mind for the rest of the afternoon.

Recess was followed by American History with Mr. Barber who was a great teacher as far as Gaspar was concerned. Instead of endless boring lectures, he had brought only one book to the class, *John Adams* by David McCullough. Each day Mr. Barber would read, and re-read chapters from the book, allowing his class to live, breath, smell and taste the 18th century in America. Gaspar had attended American History classes before but they were nothing compared to Mr. Barber's. The readings from this extraordinary book and the discussions that ensued had captivated Gaspar and the rest of the class completely. For the first time he understood viscerally the sacrifices that every man, woman and child had made in order to win freedom from the King of England and create the United States of America. Mr. Barber presented his subject in such an irresistible way that he had the entire class eating out of his hand.

English with Mrs. Laker was another story. An elegant lady with an upper class English accent, she challenged her students to speak the King's English, which they all attempted to parrot between giggles. During her lesson on *Prepositions and Phrasal Verbs*, a summons for Gaspar to appear immediately in the principal's office was delivered to the classroom.

Before he'd even opened the office door, Gaspar knew he was in trouble. Mr. Minton was a fair fellow, and had a big job as the principal of not only the junior high, but also the high school next door. He asked Gaspar what he knew about a secret society which planned to meet on Sunday nights to discuss subversive subjects.

"Not a thing, sir," Gaspar answered honestly. "But I must say it sounds like an interesting idea."

"Don't get smart with me, Mr. Brown," Minton warned him. "If you're planning something outside the school as an extracurricular activity, I need to know about it."

"I tell you what, sir," Gaspar promised, "if I do something outside of school in my own house that is something other than a private invitation to other students, I'll let you know."

"You do that, Gaspar," the principal chided. "I don't want to hear about any subversive funny business going on amongst my students."

As Gaspar left the principal's office, he saw Iilona in the hall. She was leaning against the wall near the water fountain at the corner where the two hallways intersected. Gaspar was in no mood to stop and chat, so he just nodded to her and kept on walking. He could almost feel her big black cow eyes following him down the hall.

After school, he called an emergency meeting of the club and told his twelve pals, who were sitting on the bleachers on the ball field, what had happened.

"You guys, you know it wasn't open roll call. What Alex and I planned was strictly private. Mine was a personal invitation for our friends, not for the entire island to attend, and certainly not for upper or under classmen either, and especially not for *girls*." Gaspar admonished them. "We gotta get this situation under control before we can take this idea forward. By next Sunday, I'll be able to give you an answer as to my decision. In the meantime, don't invite anyone to be your guest, till you hear back from me."

Later that day, after Auto Shop, Gaspar told Alex that he had to run some errands for his mother and that he'd call him later, after he got home. Lamar was waiting for them outside the school and Gaspar told him to take Alex wherever he wanted to go, and that he'd call later and let Lamar know where he wanted to be picked up. With that, Gaspar hightailed it up Main Street and headed straight for the Calaluna Police Station. When he got there he asked for Captain Morgan, and was soon escorted into the police chief's office.

"Good afternoon, Gaspar," Chief Morgan greeted him.

"Good afternoon, chief," Gaspar hailed his friend.

"O'Malley tells me that you had some excitement last night at La Rinconada."

"Yes, sir, my mother lost some of her jewelry to robbers. I brought you a list, with photographs and estimates attached. These were compiled by my curator, Jason Steinmeyer. Do you know Jason? He has an antique store in Llojeta during the season, and works for me at La Rinconada on Mondays and Fridays, along with my librarian, Miss Stewart. Since my cousin Eugenia had so many antiques and personal items of value I've hired Jason to make an inventory and appraisal of everything for insurance purposes. Having Jason on staff has helped me tremendously!"

"I've not met Mr. Steinmeyer, but I look forward to the opportunity one day soon," the chief informed him.

"Did Sergeant O'Malley tell you that my mother had no idea that the items that were stolen were precious? It's embarrassing, but you know my mother well, chief. I'm sure it doesn't surprise you, and like I told the sergeant, if she had any idea that the baubles were genuine, I can guarantee you she never would have agreed to wear them, let alone own them." Gaspar spilled the beans to the police chief.

"I understand completely. Knowing your mother, what you tell me doesn't surprise me at all. Of course, I also knew your dear late cousin, and am well aware of the magnificence of her collections. I think you're lucky that the thieves didn't actually get away with more," the chief mused.

"Well, captain, the truth is we actually haven't found all of cousin Eugenia's jewelry yet. That's what Jason and Margaret are helping me with. There are drawers and drawers, and secret compartments, closets, cabinets, trunks. You've seen the place. My cousin Eugenia was particularly clever about hiding her treasures. The funny thing is that some of her jewels were only copies of the real thing, and some *are* the real thing. Putting it all together has almost become a full-time job." Gaspar exclaimed sheepishly, embarrassed by his enviably lavish predicament.

"You'll get to the bottom of it, Gaspar. It sounds like you have a lot of good helpers and if you don't mind my saying so, it seems to me like a good kind of problem to have. You should be having a lot of fun with this, like a treasure hunt in your own house," Captain Morgan enthused, turning over the papers Gaspar had handed him. "This is a very complete inventory of what's been taken. My men will get on this right away. In the meantime, have you called the insurance company to file a claim?"

"Well, sir, I'd like to avoid that for the present. Peter and I think it is enough to have the police report and we have every faith that you and your men will get to the bottom of all these crimes. In the meantime, we want to avoid any undue publicity for my mother's sake. We've also doubled the guard at La Rinconada, just for good measure."

"Very smart," the captain approved. "Better safe than sorry."

"That's what my mom always says. Well thank you for your help Captain Morgan. If there's anything else you need from us, please just let me or Peter know." Gaspar smiled as he got up and extended the police chief his hand. On his way out the door, Gaspar stopped to ask one last question. "Captain Morgan, can you tell me where the Seminole Spring is?" It occurred to Gaspar that the captain would surely know ins and outs of the island.

"The Seminole Spring, is that a health club or something?" Captain Morgan asked, to Gaspar's surprise.

"No, sir, it's a place somewhere around here where my friend Iilona lives." Gaspar explained.

"I'm sorry, Gaspar. Off the top of my head, I can't place it. But why don't you ask her for directions. It's got to be around here someplace. To be perfectly honest, I've never heard of it," the captain confessed, "but I'll ask around for you and find out."

"Okay, captain, that would be great. But don't go to any trouble." Gaspar let the subject drop. "I'll be seeing ya, sir."

CHAPTER 8

LEGAL ADVICE

THAT AFTERNOON, WHEN GASPAR GOT BACK TO LA RINCONADA, HE WAS HAPPY TO SEE THAT PETER Cawthorne was there visiting Elvira.

"Hello, baby," Elvira called from the terrace where they were seated.

"Hi, mom. Hi, Peter," Gaspar called back, walking onto the terrace through the French doors of the living room.

"How was school today?" his mother asked innocently.

"Oh, ma. It was the worse," Gaspar let loose. "You know my plan for a social club that I wanted to put together in Llojeta. Well … word got out about it and I was inundated with kids who all wanted to join, or who couldn't understand why they weren't invited to join. It was a mess and even Mr. Minton got wind of all the talk and called me into his office. He accused me of creating some kind of a secret society to discuss subversive ideas outside of school."

"Welcome to the real world, Gasp," Peter stroked Gaspar's wounded ego. "Just remember, *no good deed goes unpunished.*"

"That's what Uncle Charlie said!" Gaspar blurted out, without thinking.

"What was that, *Uncle Charlie?*" Elvira picked up on what Gaspar had let slip.

"I meant, I saw that written down somewhere in some of Uncle Charlie's papers that I found in my room," Gaspar fibbed.

"Oh," his mother said absent-mindedly. "What are you going to do, Gaspar? Close it down?"

"Ma, I haven't even had my first event yet," Gaspar protested. "I'm not gonna close it down, that's for sure. Peter, can you help me out. I'm lost on this one." Gaspar pleaded with his lawyer.

"It's simple, Gaspar … in one word … *invitations.*"

"What?"

"Send out invitations. That way it's private. If you want them to bring friends, then you can stipulate it on the invitation. If you are having a special guest speaker, or a dancing instructor, or screening a special old movie … put it on the invitation. These don't have to be fancy engraved invitations, just emailed, or printed on regular typing paper, and specify RSVP and *non-transferable*. That way you'll be home free with the principal and everyone else at school. Remember, Gasp, there's always *more than one way to skin a cat*."

"Thanks, Peter. That was easy. I'll get right on it," Gaspar said, jumping up and heading for his office. "I like the way you think."

"Glad I could help, Gasp," Peter smiled.

"By the way, Peter," Gaspar turned back toward his friend. "You grew up here. Do you know where the Seminole Spring is?"

"The Seminole Spring. No, can't say that I've ever heard of it. What is it, or how did you hear about it?" the lawyer asked.

"Oh, a friend of mine at school. Her name's Iilona and she wants me to go there and meet her mother and grandma," Gaspar tried shrugging it off.

"That serious, huh?" Peter joked.

"Cut it out, Peter, I hardly know the girl. She's kind-a weird, a loner. She even dresses funny, but I think it might be because she's poor. I don't know, but next time I see her, I'll ask her where the Seminole Spring is. Maybe it's on the mainland."

"Maybe," Peter cut in. "I sure as heck haven't heard of it. the Seminole Spring, I'll look into it a little more when I get back to the office," he promised.

"Don't bother, Peter. Lamar's never heard of it either. No one around here has. It's gotta be across the bridge, on the other side." Gaspar let the subject drop.

Leaving the adults on the terrace, Gaspar strode through the living room towards the library. When he got there he found Margaret Stewart, his librarian working on the stacks.

"Margaret, I need your help. Please drop everything and give me a hand. I need to find out about the Seminole Spring and where it is."

"The Seminole Spring, what's that, a fruit juice bar?" Margaret asked, picking up a collector's copy of the local Yellow Pages and starting to flip through the listings.

"No, no ... it's a place, a neighborhood, here on Perdido Isle. I have a friend who lives there. I need to find out where it is. It's important," Gaspar wailed, completely exasperated.

"Calm down, sir," Margaret begged. "If it exists, I'll find it. Give me some time, and I'll get back to you with an answer. The Seminole Spring, hmmm, the Seminole Spring. It seems somehow familiar. Please, go away and leave me alone and I'll do my best. I'll tell you the minute I come up with something." She reassured her young boss.

CHAPTER 9

R.S.V.P.

T HE NEXT DAY GASPAR HANDED OUT INVITATIONS TO THE TWELVE CHARTER MEMBERS OF HIS SOCIAL CLUB. The invitation was for the following weekend. It stated that each boy was invited to bring one guest for a day of fun and games, with lunch and dinner included. The invitation stated that Gaspar expected at least one parent to accompany each guest. Gaspar couldn't wait to meet their parents and introduce them to Mrs. Hobart. He also looked forward to showing them around Villa Gaspar. He made it clear that the day would end promptly at 9:30 pm right after the screening of his favorite MGM film, *The Broadway Melody of 1936* starring Robert Taylor, Eleanor Powell, Una Merkel, Sid Silvers, Buddy Ebsen and Jack Benny. He suggested that they should bring appropriate attire for swimming, weight lifting

73

and calisthenics and also stipulated that the attire for dinner would be coat and tie. He left his email address, gasparbrown@larinconada.com, so that his friends could *RSVP* and asked that they let him know the name of the guest they planned to bring.

Gaspar couldn't wait to see what would happen. Sure enough practically every one of the boys asked him what *RSVP* stood for. Most of the guys wanted to know if it was some kind of secret *code*, required for entrance to the private club.

"No, you *sub-product of ectoplasm*," Gaspar would holler. "Haven't your parents taught you anything. RSVP stands for *respondez s'il vous plait*, which in French means please respond and let me know if you're coming and if you're bringing a friend so that I can order enough food for you and be prepared to receive you … *you stupid, cachinnating Cro-Magnon cockatoo*," he proudly *Captain Haddocked* twice in one response.

"Oh. I get it. Okay, Gasp, I'll *respondez s'il vous …* whatever you call it. I'll send you an email" was what practically every one of his pals said, and they did.

Gaspar figured that his response was reasonable and that nobody would ever ask him again what *RSVP* meant. He later had to laugh when the next day *RSVP* became the most used phrase at Jackson Junior High.

After school, Gaspar had a long-standing date with Elvira and Peter over at The Perdido Isle Historical Society Museum. It was a notable day for all three of them, when the board of directors of the museum asked Elvira and Peter to join the board, and voted young Gaspar as their new president. After the shake-up of the summer, where the executive director Gwendolyn Crump had been jailed for grand theft amongst other transgressions, many of the original board had resigned, leaving space for new members who would prudently guide the organization soundly into the new century.

After the meeting at the museum, Peter and Gaspar raced back to Peter's office to work with Brewster Wharton, his new law clerk, who was up to his ears trying to figure out how to minimize the inheritance taxes which Gaspar owed the government. All kinds of suggestions were afoot to donate land and valuable objects to the museum as a means of settling cousin Eugenia's estate. When they arrived at the office, Jason Steinmeyer and Margaret Stewart were also waiting for them.

It had been after one of these lengthy meetings several weeks ago that Gaspar had asked Margaret Stewart, who was not only the museum's librarian, but its official historian, if all the objects in the museum were the property of the museum or just on loan from generous patrons. She answered Gaspar's question in no uncertain terms.

"All of the exhibits in the museum and the books in the library, every stick of furniture right down to the file cabinets in the offices were the property of Charles

Munoz-Flores y Gaspar, your late great-great-uncle," Margaret revealed with relish.

At the time, Gaspar was speechless, as well as exhilarated by this revelation.

Peter, on the other hand was dismayed. "That only makes your inheritance even larger and more taxable, Gaspar. A complete inventory will need to be compiled." Peter shook his head wearily at the thought of all the extra work and expense.

"I'll have Jason get right on it," Gaspar offered. "He loves nothing better than scrounging around in museums."

When Gaspar told Jason what he needed, Jason jumped at the chance to work on the inventory. "I'll give you a daily report in writing," he promised. Soon a very thick book of photographs with descriptions had turned into 24 volumes with values adding up to several millions of dollars.

At today's meeting, Gaspar had another revelation that he figured Peter would be none too pleased to hear. "Peter, I hate to bring this up, but I bet you a dollar, the same is true at the iglesia as at the Historical Society Museum." Gaspar told the lawyer.

"What do you mean by the same is true at the iglesia?"

"Just that it seems logical to me that Uncle Charlie only loaned all that stuff to Saint Anna's church. I bet it really belongs to me," Gaspar said, without pulling any punches.

"Where there's smoke, there's fire, Gaspar. Margaret, what do you think?" Peter asked the historian.

"Exactly that … it's all just borrowed. Somewhere around La Rinconada I'll find the document that the Catholic church signed to that effect." Margaret filled Peter in innocently.

"Oh, brother. Okay, let's look into it. But we can't send Jason over there right now. First we need to find the document, and then I'll inform Bishop du Bon Secours regarding the lay of the land. That's gonna be a lot of fun!" Peter's voice belied his true feelings on the subject.

Leaving Jason, Margaret, Peter and Brewster the unhappy job of unwinding the tangled web of almost a hundred years of Uncle Charlie's generous loans, Gaspar left to find Alex and plan some more fun and games with their pals.

CHAPTER 10

POLICE BUSINESS

Amidst all Gaspar's activitiy in and out of school, Iilona had inexplicably disappeared and as hard as he tried to find her, she was nowhere in sight. On top of that, no matter how many people he asked, Gaspar couldn't find out anything about her or where The Seminole Spring was located. Because Iilona had dropped off the face of the earth, Gaspar let other more immediate things fill his mind and his days. Thoughts of Iilona and The Seminole Spring were replaced by school activities, sports and keeping up with the ongoing news regarding the continuing crime spree that had spread up and down the Gulf Coast between Pensacola and Naples. More importantly, the police had been unable to discover anything to do with the theft of Elvira's jewelry, nor the whereabouts of the magnificent jewels of Señora

Martinez de Gozz. Each day brought new horror stories of break-ins, hold-ups and robberies of all kinds, a lot of them centering on tiny Perdido Isle itself. For the past month Gaspar had put La Rinconada on lockdown, hiring an extra night watchman to help Ramon on his regular rounds, securing the property. Although the crime spree seemed contained within a narrow strip of Florida coastline, law enforcement hadn't been able to pinpoint the gang's hideout or who their ringleader was. Gaspar had consulted informally with his pals Captain Morgan and Sergeant O'Malley at the Calaluna Police Station about the irregular goings on, but neither of the men could shed any further light on what had been spoiling the high times in the resort town of Llojeta this season.

After hearing reports of a particularly messy robbery involving the severe beating of an elderly businessman up in Coral County, Gaspar came to and called Captain Morgan asking for an appointment. That afternoon Gaspar had Lamar drive him into town … telling him to wait in the car outside the precinct. The minute Gaspar walked through the door, Sergeant O'Malley escorted him directly into Captain Morgan's office.

"Gaspar, good to see you," welcomed the captain. "How can I help you today?"

"Captain, I just wanted to ask you a couple of questions about the robbery of Señora Martinez de Gozz.

I've read all the papers, but I thought I'd come by to clarify a few things."

"All right, Gaspar. Anything I can do to enlighten you … shoot," the captain acquiesced.

"Captain, is it true that the Martinez de Gozz robbery was done by five men wearing colorful sports clothes, like fancy golf clothes?"

"Yes, but nobody knows this other than the victim, not even the hotel manager. In fact the only ones privy to this information are the robbers, Señora de Gozz and the police," Captain Morgan spewed in confusion.

"Did they drive up to the service entrance of the hotel in a late model royal blue sedan, with one of the men staying behind the wheel with the engine running, and did he actually turn the car around so that the front faced the driveway going out?"

"But, Gaspar, that is our supposition. How did you know? Who've you been talking to?" The captain was outwardly agitated.

"It's not a supposition, captain. That's actually how it happened," Gaspar informed the astounded policeman.

"I don't understand," the captain pondered what the kid was telling him. "What else have you heard?"

"Did the four men enter The Grande Hotel Floride through the service entrance and take the service elevator up to the tenth floor, walking directly to the Ambassador Suite, number 1025, the big two-bedroom suite facing the Gulf with two terraces, one on the north side and the other on the south side?"

"Gaspar, where are you getting all this classified information? I'll get to the bottom of this leak, so you may as well tell me now," the captain insisted.

Gaspar ignored his friend's agitated question and continued. "Did they really enter the suite using a pass key, surprising Señora Martinez de Gozz and her lady's maid? Did they actually tie the lady up with her own Hermes silk scarf, and did they actually gag her with a pretty pink handkerchief with lace insets embroidered with her initials?"

"Gaspar, enough!" shouted the visibly shaken police captain.

"Were they actually able to open her safe without the slightest difficulty by dialing 25 right, 38 left and 93 right and help themselves to all of her sparklers, including a magnificent jeweled dagger and a pendant diamond that she told you was the first cutting of the *Koh-i-noor*?" Gaspar finished up matter-of-factly without ever blinking an eye, just like Iilona had when she'd told him the same implausible story.

Captain Morgan seemed exhausted by Gaspar's diatribe. He asked, "Gaspar, how do you know all of these details? Who have you been talking to?"

Gaspar just smiled and said, "I got it first hand. I also heard that they tied up her lady's maid using the strings from her apron, and gagged her with one of her own white cotton gloves. She's a French girl, if I'm not mistaken. I heard that she was very upset. The French aren't accustomed to so much excitement."

"Okay, spill the beans, Gaspar. What do you know that I don't know?" Captain Morgan implored.

"Not right this minute, captain. Let me get back to my source and find out how she knew all those details."

"She … ? Are you telling me that a woman was involved in that heist?" Captain Morgan nearly jumped out from behind his desk.

"No, captain. But I know a girl who knows more about this than any of us. Let me talk with her and get back to you. By the way, captain, were you able to find out anything about the Seminole Spring?"

"No, I asked around, but nobody here has ever heard of it," Captain Morgan confessed, exasperated that his conversation with Gaspar was going around in circles.

"I promise to get back to you, captain. Right now I've got work to do," Gaspar said, extricating himself from the chief's office and heading out to the waiting car.

"Home, Lamar. I need to do some research," Gaspar ordered.

CHAPTER II

THE FIRST MEETING

Gaspar had asked his mother and Peter to drive him over to Llojeta, right after Sunday mass at Saint Anna's to help him greet his guests. He made sure that Alex came with Felix and Angela, so that there were no exceptions to his invitation. Arriving at Villa Gaspar, Mrs. Hobart greeted her boss, his mother and her fiancé, Peter Cawthorne. Soon the other boys arrived and sheepishly introduced their parents to Gaspar. He in turn introduced his mother, stepfather-to-be and Mrs. Hobart to his pals and their parents. Soon the house was filled with boisterous teenagers and their parents who they enthusiastically introduced to each other as they showed each other around the house. After an hour, Gaspar thanked the parents for stopping by and taking his hint, the parents finally departed, leaving the boys to

85

enjoy their new *Sunday Club*. The day went very smoothly, and everyone did whatever they felt like. Gaspar and Mrs. Hobart told the boys that locker rooms had been set up in the old servant's wing off the kitchen and that the first room and bath were for guests holding invitations, and that the second room was reserved for their guests.

The twelve boys who had been invited as guests were a varied crew including Tucker Marks, who was invited by Gaspar and was a little on the chubby side. Gaspar liked Tucker because he had been so welcoming on his first day at school and had such a great sense of humor.

Alex had invited Chad Howard, who Gaspar liked because Chad never stopped smiling.

Walker Phillips, who came with Kevin was tall and thin and very serious. Gaspar had not met him previously and looked forward to knowing Walker better.

Sancho's pal, Herbert Jefferson Jr., was the son of Gaspar's friend Herbert Jefferson who drove the Perdido Isle bus between the two towns on the island. A tall, thin athletic teenager, Herbert was the star of the Jackson basketball team. Gaspar was glad to have the popular boy at the first meeting of the *Sunday Club*.

Mark's friend, Ernesto Lopez was a good-looking Latino boy who was short and stocky and a great soccer player. Gaspar didn't know him, but looked forward to learning more about Ernesto and his other interests.

Pat had invited Mario Marino, the son of the fancy Italian grocer in Llojeta. A good- looking Latin type with olive skin and dark features, Pat had told Gaspar that Mario was the heartthrob of all the girls in junior high.

Kenny Lew, a boy of Chinese descent, was the school's honor student and had been invited by Jimmy Townsend *to give some brains to the assemblage,* as Jimmy had said. Kenny's pop was supposed to be a financial whiz who worked as a private banker at the Perdido Isle Bank in Llojeta, but the family lived in a big house in Calaluna.

Also invited to attend the first meeting as a guest was another Asian fellow, Tony Lee, who had been invited by Frank Cassidy.

Roger La Mont was a new student at Jackson. His family had moved to Calaluna over the summer, around the same time that Gaspar and Elvira had. The LaMonts had come from Alabama, and Roger's dad worked for the Florida State Board of Equalization. Roger had been invited by Tommy Sullivan. Gaspar secretly wondered how well he would fit in with the gang.

Reginald Philpot, a roly-poly English boy with an exaggerated upper class accent, had been invited by Tim Scanlan. From what Gaspar knew, Reginald always seemed to have his nose in a book. What Gaspar wanted to know was what kinds of books Reginald liked best.

Louis White had invited Brian Weinstein, whose grandfather had been a successful clothing manufacturer in New York. His father was the well-to-do rabbi at the Temple Emanuel in Llojeta.

Last but not least, Travis had invited the most exotic boy in school, Jeremy Whiteleather, whose mother and father were both Seminole. The first thing Gaspar asked him when they met was if Jeremy knew where the Seminole Spring was, but Jeremy didn't have a clue.

"Lunch will be served at one o'clock," Gaspar announced. "I think by now most of you know the lay of the land here, and if you don't, the guy who invited you can fill you in."

Without too much pushing or shoving or any type of organization the kids broke up into groups and scattered. Gaspar chose to keep to himself for the time being, just to see what would happen. Moving from room to room, he found the drawing room and the dining room deserted. Anthony had discovered the library and was happily perusing the various volumes all by himself. Gaspar asked him how he liked the selection and Anthony silently approved by shaking his head with delight. Not wanting to disturb the young Englishman, Gaspar continued on his tour. Across the hall, the media room was empty. The next room was the billiard room where he found Kevin, Mario, Jimmy and Tony battling over a competitive game of 8-ball. The game room had a table of four Monopoly players including Alex, Travis, Tim and Ernesto, rolling the dice for real estate, while checkers were being played at another table between Walker and Tucker. Passing through the service porch into the former servants' wing, Gaspar checked out the locker rooms and found Chad and Sancho changing into gym clothes, getting ready to head outside. When he got to the pub room, he wasn't surprised to see it deserted too. When he stepped out into the garden, he found Jeremy, Brian, Louis, Roger and Frank splashing around in the pool, jumping out and diving back in, while Kenny and Pat worked on their tans and gabbed on the sidelines. Inside the pool house, Mark and Herbert were busy lifting weights, as Chad and Sancho walked in to join them. Very interesting, Gaspar thought to himself, seeing the interaction of his friends.

In the two hours that passed before Mrs. Hobart announced lunch, Gaspar watched the entire situation change. Boys who had been in the pool had moved to the gym equipment, and those that had worked out in the gym had moved to the steam room. A few of the swimmers had moved to the sidelines to catch some sun while those on the sidelines had moved to the pool, floating around on the rafts resembling giant alligators which Alex and Gaspar had purchased online. Reginald Philpot had never left the library and was happy as a clam, reading a biography of young Abraham Lincoln. Meanwhile the Monopoly game had wound down with Alex coming out the winner, holding all the best properties and all of the other players' money, leaving Travis and Tim bankrupt and Ernesto holding four railroads and nothing else. When Ernesto landed on Alex's Park Place Hotel, the game was officially over. It had cost

Ernesto all of his railroads plus what little cash he had left just to pay for one night at Alex's fancy address. Walker and Tucker had long since given up on their game of checkers, and were now hanging out in the billiard room, having joined in on a new game of pool with Kevin and Jimmy, while Mario and Tony challenged each other to a game of chess.

When lunch was finally announced by Mrs. Hobart, the boys didn't need any encouragement to come forward. Lunch was casual and the table was surrounded by boys in trunks, gym shorts and t-shirts, while some still had on the same clothes they'd arrived in. As before, it was a self-serve meal where everything had been laid out in the kitchen as a buffet. Because there were so many kids today, Mrs. Hobart had brought in reinforcements, with Lamar Washington and his wife, Cora helping out. Gaspar was pleased to see his friends eat with gusto, as Mrs. Hobart's selection of sandwiches, salads, chips and cookies seemed to hit the spot. Lamar offered soft drinks, milk, water and iced tea. Gaspar was pleased to see how politely his friends, following his lead, thanked the help for their service.

After lunch was over, nobody asked anybody else what they wanted to do … they just did it. Gaspar decided to join in the fun, and moved with the flow from the pool to the steam room, from the library to the game room. Time flew by and at four, like clockwork, all the guys assembled in the pub where Gaspar and Alex helped make sundaes and sodas, shakes, malts and banana splits for their friends. The guys went at the fountain like pros, heaping on the different types of ice creams, and laughing over all the amazing toppings which Mrs. Hobart had provided. Lamar took up a position by the door, lest someone need something that somehow had been left out of the mix. Without any conscious effort the boys broke into groups, sitting around eating, drinking and laughing, while another group took up a rip-roaring round of darts.

When the clock in the pub struck six, Gaspar clinked his sundae glass and got everyone's attention. "Listen guys, it's six o'clock. Dinner will be at six-thirty in the dining room, and as you all know, we are dressing. So this is the moment of truth. Let's get going, cause we don't want to keep Mrs. Hobart waiting."

Without any argument the guys pushed and shoved and laughed their way towards the locker rooms. Most of the guys had showered after their swims or workouts, but those who hadn't, did so using the facilities provided. Gaspar had planned ahead and provided combs and toothbrushes, toothpaste and mouthwash, as well as hair gel, razors, shaving cream and aftershave lotion too, even though none of his friends had started shaving yet. A few, like Kevin and Sancho, showed off by pretending that they needed to shave before dinner. There were plenty of benches in the locker rooms and mirrors for the boys to dress in front of, and although it was a little crowded, the atmosphere was festive and a lot of them got a good laugh out of seeing their pals dressed up for the first time. Just as Gaspar had figured, it was a bonding experience to say the least.

Mrs. Hobart clanged the old gong, which had come with the house, with its elegant raised gold and blue-painted chinoiserie decoration. Hearing the gong, everyone knew that dinner was served. In a pack, the boys scurried towards the dining room, leaving a few still struggling with their ties as they raced forward. Just as they arrived in the entrance hall, with Gaspar and Alex in the lead, Lamar opened the sliding mahogany doors, revealing the beautiful candle-lit room. Many of the boy's present had never seen anything as magnificent, not even in the movies. Gaspar, of course, had thought of everything and had arranged the friends around the table, using place cards. He had purposefully not placed guests next to those who had invited them, so that he could watch their interactions with the others.

Mrs. Hobart had prepared a great dinner. The first course was a delicious tomato and red pepper soup, served with pumpernickel cheese toast. Gaspar took note of how many of his pals slurped their soup unnecessarily, and which ones tipped the soup bowls forward instead of backwards. After Lamar and Cora cleared the soup dishes, Mrs. Hobart offered a platter of roast beef, roasted potatoes and green beans mixed with bits of bacon and sautéed shallots. Gaspar watched Lamar proffer the silver platter from the left and watched his friends' discomfort at trying to serve themselves, using the silver utensils Mrs. Hobart had provided. He also took note of which of his gentlemen friends were able to handle the situation while still carrying on a conversation with their table partners, and which ones on the other hand quipped with Lamar, which Gaspar was not amused by at all.

Watching his friends eat was another matter entirely. Gaspar wanted to cry when he saw the way some of the boys held their knives, *as if they were planning to plunge it into some enemy's heart* rather than to easily slice off a small enough bite to fit into their mouths. The same was true with the forks, which he noticed looked like they were *wielding a pitchfork* rather than a fine silver table utensil. Watching the mutilation of Mrs. Hobart's elegant haricot verts also made him want to cry … with laughter. He was going to have some fun turning these *un-muzzled, sheep-biting rats-banes* into elegant men of the world. No matter how hard he tried, not verbally but by theatrically performing the task over and over again, he couldn't get six of them to remove the napkin from the left side of their dish and place it onto their laps. No matter how many times he made a show of picking his napkin up to wipe his mouth, then dramatically placing it back down on his lap with a flourish, could he get their attention. Gaspar decided his efforts to teach by his own actions was more than ludicrous, it was *hopeless*.

For this inaugural evening, Gaspar had ordered a simple dinner. He wasn't trying to break the bank or show off, and even if he had been trying to do so, he now doubted if it would have made any difference one way or the other to the *currish, crook-pated clowns* she'd assembled around his table. Mrs. Hobart had made a version of Raspberries Romanoff for dessert, which she placed in front of Gaspar, who served it on Uncle Charlie's really elegant hand painted dessert dishes. Lamar offered whipped cream from a large silver bowl, going from guest to guest, after Mrs. Hobart had placed their desserts in front of them. Gaspar loved Raspberries Romanoff and had found a recipe for it from Romanoff's Restaurant in Hollywood in one of Uncle Charlie's old files.

During dinner, Gaspar told his guests, "I want to use this dining room to have roundtable discussions about current events and popular interests.

"Give us an example, *captain*," Kevin spoke up.

"Okay, let's talk about illegal immigration," Gaspar offered. "We'll go around the table starting with Alex and see where we end up. Alex, do you think that the United States government should offer citizenship to illegal aliens before granting citizenship to immigrants who have stood in line for ten years?"

The entire table went silent, as all eyes turned towards Alex.

"I think that we should give illegal aliens green cards right this minute so that we can start collecting their taxes," Alex started the ball rolling.

"Why do we need them to pay taxes?" Tucker asked.

"Because they use all our facilities, our parks, our hospitals, our schools, but they have no skin in the game," Chad insisted.

"But these are not rich people. What if they can't afford to pay taxes?" Sancho added.

"My dad says that poor people don't pay taxes anyway, so that's not an issue. When was the last time you heard of a poor person who was refused food, shelter or medical attention in the United States?" Kevin spewed.

"But, Kev, it's not fair to make these people wait in line. They're here. They're already part of our communities. We need to be compassionate," Jeremy cried.

"No, Jeremy. What's not fair is that my father works like a dog to put food on our table while many who are here illegally get free everything. Walker informed the table.

"If I went to any country in the world, they wouldn't let me in illegally." Mark insisted. "And if I did manage to sneak in, I'd never get free medical, food and housing. My dad's always telling me we should be putting our hard-earned tax dollars towards better education or to helping our vets, or providing incentives to small businesses to employ our own unemployed citizens."

"Mark, you've gotta have some compassion. A lot of these people are here because they can't get work in their own countries. They send their money home so that others can eat. They're not freeloaders. They're nice people and we need to help them." Pat put in his two cents.

"Yeah," said Jimmy. "My mom says we are the richest and most compassionate nation on earth. It's our duty to help others less fortunate than we are."

"Your mother's right, Jimmy. But that doesn't mean that our government has to step in and do charity work. That's the work of individuals, churches and social groups. Our tax money should be used for national defense, not for housing and feeding illegal aliens." Frank made his case.

"We don't have the money to support all these people, so if we keep up this kind of spending we'll end up just another nation at the table of nations instead of the richest." Tommy pointed out.

"What's wrong with that, Tommy? Why do we have to be the most powerful? Why can't we all just be the same?" Travis asked.

"Because we're not all the same," Lou shot back. "Sure we're all created equal, and in America we all enjoy the same inalienable equal rights. But some of us are smarter, some of us more clever, some of us can do things with our hands that others can't. Some of us can sing and perform and others of us are good with numbers. Some of us are so good-looking we can make money by just standing in front of a camera, like Mario over there." They all chuckled. "But we're not all equal in our ability to make money or have success or win a race. Those of us who dare to take chances, who aren't afraid of losing and are willing to work hard and succeed, to the degree of success we are seeking, deserve to have more than those who do not. The world isn't fair. We are all going to experience hard knocks. We're not always going to win. Life's a game and we have to play the cards we're dealt and make the most of them. I'm with Al. Give them a green card and start collecting their taxes. When they learn to read and write English, if they aren't in a gang or haven't been to jail, if they've proven themselves to be good upstanding citizens, make them legal. But they gotta stand in line like the rest of the immigrants who are coming here legally each year. There are no shortcuts in business or in life. Wait and see." Lou finished his diatribe.

Tim spoke up timidly, "I really haven't given the subject much thought. Everything that's been said makes sense to me. I can see both sides of the argument. I think this is going to take more than one dinnertime discussion to figure it all out."

Reginald spoke up. "I'm from England. My parents and I came here legally. We jumped through hoops, filled out mountains of documents and paid extremely high fees to get daddy a green card and to get resident visas for me and my mom. Great Britain was until only a short time ago one of the greatest and richest nations on earth. There was a time when the sun never set on the British Empire. And today, all we are is a nation of memories. Because England is riddled with socialism, everyone gets everything for free, and who pays for it? A small handful of hardworking Englishmen who are saddled with confiscatory taxes, so that the government can pay for those who don't want to work. In short, my former country is now bankrupt. One of our better prime ministers, Lady Thatcher put it very succinctly when she stated, *'The only thing wrong with socialism is what to do when you run out of other people's money to spend'*. I rest my case." Reginald finished with a courtly bow and a flourish of his right hand.

There followed a long silence. Then came a question from Gaspar.

"So, Reginald, what would your solution be to the problem of illegal aliens in America?"

"First you have to close the borders. You must stop the problem at the source. Then once you've got that under control, you can offer them green cards or citizenship or cherry pie, for all that matters. In England we had closed borders but then we actually invited the freeloaders in, undocumented. After that we begged them to take the money from our hardworking citizens, who, like my family, for the most part have now fled the country. You should walk down Piccadilly someday guys … It's like living in Bombay!"

"I think you are an alarmist, Reginald. You're just trying to scare us," Brian spoke up. I've met a lot of illegals and they're all very nice kids of hardworking parents."

"I don't think there's any question, Brian." Herbert joined the discussion. "My ancestors came here as slaves. My people helped build this country. Some of our masters were evil, but for the most part, slaves in America were taken care of … fed, housed, clothed and educated. In return for being taken care of, we worked. Although it may not have been ideal by today's standards, it was not much different than working for a living wage or receiving welfare or handouts from the government. In any event, I am not an African American, I am an American. I do not believe in reparation, just like Reginald. And I don't believe that all men are created equal, just like Lou thinks. I've been taught by my parents that through hard work any of us can be anything we want to be … president, billionaire, movie star … or even slave. Everything in life is our own choice and if we don't like it, we can change it. But to do that we need education, or at least the ability to read and write. Illegals who accept anything less than becoming citizens the right way are nothing more than slaves of the government, being paid to stay where they are, not to excel, not to ever be more than what they are now, a shadow society."

"Wow, Herb. I thought you were just a jock, but you've got brains. I like the way you think," Kenny complimented his friend.

"Herb, I think you're fooling yourself," Roger spoke up. "As the only other black man here, I have to disagree with you. My dad is a government worker. Thank God we can rely on the government to take care of us. Illegal aliens who live in this country deserve the same rights as all Americans. I don't see why you rich boys are making such a big deal out of this. It's not your money. It's the government's money. Get with it," Roger finished.

"Roger, what planet are you on?" Ernesto all but shouted. "It's *our* money, all of our money. Our parents aren't rich. They work hard to pay high taxes to the government, yet the government never has enough. When my parents don't have enough, we cut back. When was the last time any of you guys saw me at Karen's Cafe or at the movies? And if my clothes are looking a little tight it's cause I'm growing and they're not." Ernesto spoke up. "My dad always says it's not that we don't pay enough taxes, it's that the government spends it unwisely. Giving expensive benefits to illegal aliens and people who won't work, is not my idea of spending money wisely. My grandparents came here from Cuba as refugees and they never took a handout. My parents were born in Florida and so was I. We are all natural born American citizens and proud of it. But there's a right way to do this and a wrong way, and the government always seems to find the wrong way. This issue is more important than politics and votes. It involves the very lifeblood of our country and I for one would like to see the USA return to those golden years when the outlook on life for young people like us, was more optimistic." Ernesto finished speaking.

"I have a lot of family still living in China, and believe me an illegal alien in China wouldn't last a day." Tony told them. "Imprisonment, deportation and possibly death would be the Chinese way to handle any illegal immigrant. I think giving these people short shrift is the way to go. First close the borders, then give them green cards and put them in line. It's the only thing that makes sense."

"What about you, Mario?" Gaspar asked. "What do you have to say."

"I'm with Alex, Lou, Reginald and Tony. Close the borders, give them green cards and put them in line. My big question is, what happened to *no taxation without representation*. It seems to me that the very phrase that this country was founded on applies here. If we don't like the way the government is spending our taxes, then we should vote those representatives out and put in a group that will do what we want them to."

"And that, Kevin, is what a roundtable discussion is all about," Gaspar chuckled, pushing back his chair. "Listen guys, that was really fun and interesting. I like the way you all think. But most of all, in this house and especially at this table, I want to make sure that going forward, just like tonight, that we always treat each others points of view with consideration and respect, and that we are always polite to one another during these discussions.

What I'd like you to do is consider yourselves modern *Knights of the Round Table*. Just like those dudes at *Camelot*, chivalry should be our code. As you know, we have a screening of *The Broadway Melody of 1936* tonight. If we don't go in now and see it, we won't get out of here by 9:30, like I promised. Besides, tomorrow is a school day. So let's go into the media room and watch it. It's one of the wackiest old movies ever." Gaspar finished by way of introduction.

CHAPTER 12

THE MORNING AFTER

MONDAY STARTED OUT LIKE ANY OTHER, BUT BY THE TIME SCHOOL LET OUT, GASPAR WOULDN'T KNOW what hit him. Word of the events of the day before spread through the campus from class to class like falling dominoes and soon every boy, girl and teacher were talking about Gaspar's boys club. Illegal immigration had become the topic du jour and polite discussions broke out on the subject during every period. On top of that, all the girls who had not been invited to *Villa Gaspar* decided to take enormous offense, and the boys that had been passed over for an invitation, pretended not to care, while making their feelings known.

When Gaspar got to the cafeteria at noon, he was approached by Kevin's twin sister, June Arden. June was the most popular girl in his class and a real fox.

"Gaspar, I'm wondering if you'd like to have lunch with me?" June asked sweetly.

"Oh … golly … sure June … I'd love to," Gaspar stuttered. He'd barely ever spoken to June, let alone had lunch with her or any other girl for that matter.

"Let's sit over there," June suggested, pointing out a small table for two in the corner of the big cafeteria.

Together they took their trays and sat down. From his corner, Gaspar saw Alex frozen in his tracks with his mouth hanging open. He soon realized that the entire school was watching him and June, as if spellbound. He could hear the buzz of speculation as to what was going on, over in that corner as it reached a fever pitch. But Gaspar attempted not to notice and he was glad that June did too.

"What's on your mind, June?" Gaspar asked politely, taking a bite of his chicken sandwich.

"Well, Gaspar, everyone's talking about your *social club* and some of the girls and I were just wondering how we could get in on it?"

"Oh, sorry June … it's a gentleman's club. Guys only, you understand," Gaspar told her, uncomfortably.

"Well everyone's talking about it. Tell me how it works. I'd like to hear it from you. What's it all about? What's your goal, or is it all just fun and games for guys?" she asked seriously.

"Well, June, it was just an idea I had. You see, I inherited this big house up in Llojeta. It's just sitting there empty, all furnished and everything, and I thought it would be a good idea to put it to use for us guys, by giving us a place to hang out. You know, a place to goof off."

"That's not what I heard. Some of the boys have mentioned intellectual discussions, movie nights, guest speakers, dancing classes …"

"Oh well, those are just some hairbrained ideas of mine, June. I like old movies. I think they have a lot to teach us young folk. And I like good manners and people who are well dressed, like in the old movies and elegant parties, just like in the old movies. *Shiver me dungbie drivelswiggers*, I guess I just like old movies," Gaspar confessed only a little embarrassed.

"The girls and I think what you're doing is really important, Gaspar, if that means anything to you."

"Wha-da-ya mean, the girls and you?"

"It's true. We like you and your friends, but we're going to like you so much more when you learn to behave like gentlemen … how to dress, how to dance, how to hold a knife and fork, like you're doing right now." She complimented him. "You have so much to offer your pals. What you're doing in Llojeta is important not only for the guys but for us girls too."

"That's very interesting, June. I'm glad you see it that way," Gaspar beamed.

"Have you heard all the talk going around school today? Everyone's talking about illegal immigration. My brother told me that it started at your clubhouse last night. This is the first time I can remember when kids in school have been actually engaged in discussing an important subject. The part I like best is that they aren't just arguing different points of view but are actually listening and respecting their friend's right to express the way they feel without passing judgment. You've revived in one night what an entire nation hasn't been able to remember in a long time."

"What's that?"

"That we are all individuals and entitled to our own opinions."

"June, that's great. It's nice to know that the girls are with us on this."

"We're not only with you guys. We want to participate too. Come on Gaspar, between you and me, how can we make that happen?"

"Okay, June. Where there's a will, there's a way, and I think I can meet you half way. Here's an idea, so let's see if it works for you. How 'bout I offer you, as president of the Young Ladies Auxiliary my house, Villa Gaspar, on Wednesday afternoons. Mrs. Hobart is our house mother and she will supervise you, just like she does us. We'll set up dressing rooms for you and your friends upstairs, which is currently off limits to us guys. You can do whatever it is you ladies do, when you get together. Of course you're welcome to use the gym and the pool and the steam room too. The house would be yours on Wednesdays.

"I understand there is a ballroom there too," June fished.

"There is. What we're planning is a dinner dance once a month, just as soon as us guys learn to dance."

"Why don't we have a cotillion?" June blurted out.

"A *cotillion*, what's that?"

"Dancing class. We could bring in Adele Ryan from Naples. She teaches all the kids over there how to dance. If we could bring her in once a month to help us, it would be terrific. She also teaches table manners and deportment too."

"Yeah, but you're talking about co-ed classes. And that's not what we have in mind, me and the guys, that is." Gaspar protected his territory.

"No, Gaspar, only for the dancing, boys and girls only for the dancing. Miss Ryan can teach us together, one afternoon a month. Otherwise, we'll keep it separate. You and the guys on Sundays, me and the gals on Wednesdays and never the twain shall meet."

"I think we can work this out. We can share some of the speakers that I've planned and even open up those nights to the entire community … I think the ballroom will hold at least four hundred guests, but I'll have to double check. Why don't you come with me after school today and check the place out. After you've seen it you may not like the set up, you know."

"Okay, that'll be great. Will you drive me?"

"Sure, meet me out in front after school, no problem," Gaspar enthused. This was going to be fun, Gaspar thought. Talking with June had been an eye-opening revelation. Girls weren't that much different to talk to than guys. He wondered what all the fuss was about.

When he regrouped with Alex, he got an earful. "Thanks a lot for ruining my lunch pal," Alex complained. "Me and the guys could barely eat a bite. We were so engrossed watching you eating lunch with a girl … *alone*. Did you like it?"

"Yeah, Al. June is great," Gaspar smiled, walking away.

CHAPTER 13

GIRLS

THE NAMES, GASPAR AND JUNE, WERE ON EVERYONE'S
LIPS. THE ENTIRE SCHOOL WAS TALKING ABOUT THE
lunch date that they'd all witnessed. Speculation about
Gaspar and June *going steady* passed from group to group
like wildfire.

"Hey man, care to talk about it?" Alex asked Gaspar,
as they left the cafeteria.

Gaspar knew better than to tell Alex anything until
it was set in stone, less what he and June had discussed
be repeated all over school and taken out of context. If
that were to happen, not only would people talk, but be
they'd also be disappointed with the outcome.

"I've asked her out," Gaspar lied. "We have a date for
this afternoon, Al. Would you mind hitching a ride back
to La Rinconada on the bus?"

"You're going to miss Auto Shop ... for a girl?" Alex asked in disbelief.

"Just for today, Al. Don't get nervous, I'm not falling for her. I don't think. But if I do, you'll be the first to know. I'll tell you all about it later. We'll talk tonight, back home," Gaspar promised.

The minute the bell signaling the end of class sounded, Gaspar grabbed his books and headed for the curb, with Alex hot on his heels. Leaving Al in the dust, he ran outside and found June waiting on the sidewalk. Lamar was parked in the usual place but instead of the old woody station wagon, Gaspar had called ahead and asked him to bring the limo. Alex couldn't believe his eyes as he watched Gaspar help June into the back of the big car. Gaspar was embarrassed when he looked out the back window to see Alex and what looked like the entire school watching open-mouthed, as he and June sped off in the direction of Llojeta. Even Iilona who he hadn't laid eyes on in a long time was standing there in the middle of the huge crowd just watching ... as usual.

"This is such an impressive car, Gaspar," June took notice.

"I thought it more appropriate for a lady. So much nicer than the old woody that Alex and I usually tool around town in."

"Alex is your best friend, isn't he?" June asked.

"Yeah, he's the first friend I made after moving here from California," Gaspar admitted proudly.

"And that's how you met my twin brother, Kevin," June said, "through Alex."

"That's right. It was on June 11th, my birthday. We played water polo with Kevin and a lot of the other guys."

"Down at the old swimmin' hole," June giggled.

"Yeah." Gaspar blushed. "Now don't tell me you want to bring your girlfriends there, cause it's off limits, guys only. Since it's on private property and I own it, I can call the shots." Gaspar threw all his weight into the argument.

"Skinny dipping isn't for us gals, Gaspar. Your precious swimmin' hole will not be violated by any dainty nymphs," June joked, "even though it might make things more interesting around there if we did come by one Saturday."

"June, don't even joke about it. I'm gonna have enough explaining to do just getting you into the clubhouse on Wednesdays."

Gaspar saw Lamar give him a surprised look in the rear view mirror, but attempted to ignore the man's reaction to hearing about girls at Villa Gaspar.

"Tell me about Iilona," Gaspar asked June, as he considered pushing the button to raise the glass between them and the driver, but then decided against it.

"Who?" June asked.

"You know, Iilona. The Seminole girl with the braids and the beige shift trimmed in gingham," Gaspar insisted.

"She's not in our class?" June asked, "because I don't know anyone by that name or description, Gaspar … and I know all the girls at school."

"You've gotta be kidding," Gaspar blurted out. "Iilona, she's like a loner. She's always standing to the side, or sitting in the back of the room. She's a Seminole Indian, she told me so herself. She lives at the Seminole Spring. You know where that is don't you, June?"

"Gaspar, I'm sorry. I know every girl in our class and even the girls in the upper and lower grades, and I don't know a Seminole Indian girl with braids and a beige and gingham trimmed shift named Iilona. What's her last name?"

"I don't know. She never told me her last name, but June, she's all over the place. She's always seeking me out, wants to take me to her house to meet her mother and her grandmother."

"Yikes, did you ask her to marry you or something?" June joked.

"Don't be funny, June. I'm serious. This girl is really strange. Now you've got me scared. Maybe she's not even supposed to be in our school, maybe she's from the mainland. Lamar, do you think the Seminole Spring is on the mainland?" he called to the driver from the back seat.

Lamar didn't answer but just shook his head *no* in the rearview mirror for Gaspar to see.

"Okay, this is really weird, June. I'll get to the bottom of it, and tomorrow I'll introduce you to Iilona. She's really very nice, but I think because of the way she dresses she may be very poor. June, I want you to be her friend and take her under your wing, and especially invite her to the girls' club on Wednesdays!" Gaspar insisted as the car pulled into the driveway at Villa Gaspar.

Gaspar escorted June up the front steps. He'd already alerted Mrs. Hobart earlier by cell phone that he would be arriving with a lady guest, and that he would like her to sit in on their conversation.

Mrs. Hobart was at the door and opened it wide as they approached the front porch.

"Good afternoon, Mr. Brown."

"Good afternoon, Mrs. Hobart. May I present my friend, June Arden. June is Kevin Arden's twin sister."

"I'm very pleased to meet you, Miss Arden," Mrs. Hobart sang. "May I offer you refreshments," she asked, turning to Gaspar.

"How about some tea, Mrs. Hobart. Does that sound good to you, June?" he asked.

"Tea would be very nice, Mrs. Hobart. Thank you very much."

"I'm going to show Miss Arden around the house. Let's serve tea on the terrace, Mrs. Hobart," Gaspar suggested.

"Very well, sir," Mrs. Hobart agreed, as she stepped out of the room and headed for the kitchen.

Gaspar proceeded to show June the house, just as he had done with her brother and his other friends.

"This is the drawing room, June. It's the original décor that my great uncle hired Elsie de Wolfe to create for him. I've made it very clear to the guys that I like it just the way it is and that I want them to respect it as if it were their own house."

"I understand, Gaspar. I would feel the same way too if I owned an original Elsie de Wolfe interior. It's a wonderful sitting room," June complimented him.

"This is the dining room," Gaspar led on. "We can have twenty-four for dinner like we did last night. We like to use the room like we did last night for roundtable discussions where everyone is polite and considerate of each other's opinions. I have beautiful dishes and silver here, everything that's needed to entertain properly," Gaspar let her know.

"It would be wonderful for us to be able to do the same, and share ideas and invite speakers who could address subjects of interest to young ladies," June enthused. "You have to understand, Gaspar, for a lot of our classmates, even the girls, this may be the first time they've ever seen such a beautifully appointed room. For them it will be a revelation and we could have flower arranging classes and lessons on how to set a proper table for every type of occasion. For us gals, life is all about the art of living and the living arts," she explained sweetly.

Gaspar couldn't have agreed with her more, but far be it for him to admit it to her. "This is the library. We have it set up the way we want it, all boys stuff. We don't want to change it so let's just agree to place this room off limits on Wednesdays. If you'd like a library or reading room, we can make one for you upstairs," Gaspar suggested.

"Hold on, Gaspar, that's silly. Since when are important subjects exclusive to only boys or girls. I understand your wishes, but this time I think you should reconsider. You've got plenty of shelf space available down here. Let's make one side of the room for boys and one side of the room for girls and the other two sides mixed. I bet you ten dollars that you'll find boys reading books from the girl's side and vice-a-versa. This will be the greatest learning experience for all of us. Boys need to know what makes a girl tick, and girls need to know what makes a boy tick. Do we have a bet?"

"June, I think you've got something there. The way I had the library set up was way too limiting for us guys. You don't have a bet, you have a deal. Work with my librarian at La Rinconada, Margaret Stewart, and you'll get the reading materials that you want. Margaret is a wizard." June had just opened his eyes.

This is the media room. I think you'll like our selections of videos and classic movies, and if you don't, you know where the suggestion box is. This is the billiard room and this was the breakfast room but I've turned it into a game room, and the old pub room over here we've turned into a self-serve soda fountain. As you can see, we also like to play darts." He whisked her through the house.

We've turned the old servant's wing into a locker room for guys. It's off limits, if you don't mind. But I'll give you two bedrooms and two bathrooms upstairs for changing rooms, which you'll need. Mrs. Hobart lives upstairs, so we need to give her, her privacy but I don't foresee a problem. This is the terrace and the pool, and the pool house which is set up as a gym, complete with two changing rooms, two bathrooms, a dry sauna and a steam room. As they stepped out of the gym, Mrs. Hobart came out onto the terrace with a tray of tea along with a dish of tea cakes.

"Thank you, Mrs. Hobart. How really nice." Gaspar complimented his house mother.

"Such beautiful china and linens," June noted, "and your tea set. I do believe it's Georgian."

"Not only Georgian but by Paul de Lamerie, London's most important silversmith. It's dated1740." Gaspar let her know that he was also a connoisseur of beautiful things.

With that, Gaspar filled Mrs. Hobart in on the new plan for Wednesday afternoons. He also let June know that Mrs. Hobart would not tolerate any impolite behavior, alcohol or smoking on the premises. All people entering the house were the personal guests of Gaspar Brown for reasons of insurance and zoning ordinances, and that the young ladies should treat the house with the respect that they would treat their own. Mrs. Hobart also let it be known that no infringements of *her* or *Gaspar's* rules would be tolerated.

Having gotten the rules and regulations out of the way, and having enjoyed a perfectly wonderful tea, they exchanged ideas with Mrs. Hobart regarding dancing classes, etiquette classes, hair and make-up classes and fashion seminars as well as guest speakers on all manner of subjects. Gaspar, who thought like an architect, suggested that they go upstairs to see the rooms he'd selected for converting into dressing rooms for the young ladies.

Mrs. Hobart had already taken the suite of rooms at the back of the house, overlooking the gardens. She had the master suite consisting of an ample bedroom with its own dressing room and bath, as well as a huge sitting room with fireplace, and an adjoining sunroom. This led to another dressing room, which she had already converted into a small dining room. There had been a second bathroom attached, which Gaspar had turned into Mrs. Hobart's very own compact kitchenette.

That left the two front bedrooms with their own dressing rooms and baths, and six more double bedrooms lining the central hall leading down to Mrs. Hobart's apartment. It was decided that they would leave those six double bedrooms locked, and only open up the two front bedrooms as the girls' dressing rooms. Gaspar went further and suggested placing a new door at the end of the hall so that the entire front end of the house would become one big suite.

Their business concluded, Gaspar took June home so that she could get started putting her ideas together. On the ride back to Calaluna, June made another sensible suggestion.

"You know, Gaspar, there's only about thirty girls in our class at school. I know the dining room only holds twenty-four, but it's not right to invite only some girls and not others. The same is true about the boys. There's only thirty-five boys in the class. I know you can figure out a way to include all of them. You've had your first try-out, but next Sunday you really should expand your horizons."

"I have to agree with you, June. It only makes sense. When we started this thing, we kinda wanted to make it exclusive, but I can see that it's not a good idea. I'll get with Alex and expand it and you do the same with the girls. I think I can find a cabinet maker who can figure out how to expand Uncle Charlie's dining table so that we can seat forty in a pinch."

"That way it would become a school thing … just for our class. Then the upperclassmen and underclassmen can't get angry for not being included," June reasoned.

"Yeah, you're right. Just so you know … I also want to use the villa for seminars and things like that, for all the people who live here. I'm not sure yet, but I may have to charge admission for some charity or other, in order to control the crowds and not play favorites."

"Oh, Gaspar … *charity*. Let the girls handle the charity part of this. It's a wonderful idea … *The Young Ladies Auxiliary*. We can help support a lot of good causes around here. Let me do that. I'd love to be in charge of that," June begged.

"June, haven't you figured it out yet. You're already in charge of everything, even me. You just turned my *man cave* into a co-ed school club … a veritable extension of Andrew Jackson Junior High."

"Yes, but Gaspar, think about it. This club can follow us, our generation, right up through high school and even into our college and married years."

"Let's not get ahead of ourselves, June. And I'll thank you to keep the '*M*' word out of anything to do with our clubhouse," Gaspar chuckled. "Here's your house. See you later, June. I'm glad we got together on this one," Gaspar said, as he helped her out of the car while Lamar held the door. "Do me a favor and don't mention this to anyone until I can tell the guys what the drill is gonna be from now on. Let's agree to have you gals start the Wednesday after next. That will give me time to get your dressing rooms pulled together, and the dining room too."

CHAPTER 14

SHALL WE DANCE?

As SEPTEMBER TURNED INTO OCTOBER, WITH THE GIRLS HOLDING COURT ON WEDNESDAY AFTERNOONS, and the boys taking over all day on Sundays, Gaspar's class was having the time of their lives at *Villa Gaspar*. Gaspar had already brought in instructors to teach both the boys and the girls important tips on personal grooming, table manners and other social graces on top of the usual swimming, board games, old movies and all around hysterical fun they had there.

At the end of October, the school gave a dance to celebrate Halloween, with all the kids invited to come in costume. Gaspar promised to dress his pals Kevin, Mark, Pat, Sancho and Alex in costumes from La Rinconada's fancy dress baskets, which were full of amusing get-ups. A week before the big night, all the boys gathered in the green bedroom of the big house, and together they rummaged through the huge wicker hampers filled with Uncle Charlie's mixed bag of mismatched paraphernalia.

Gaspar chose to dress as a Seminole Indian brave, complete with fringed doeskin pants, war paint, and feathered headdress. Alex chose to dress as a cowboy, Gaspar's polar opposite. Alex's costume was an embroidered black and white affair complete with bandana, and six shooters that he wore low on his hips. Gnarly cowboy boots complete with spurs, a pair of woolly chaps and a cool Stetson hat gave Alex an authentic air. Kevin selected a "Cat and the Fiddle" costume, complete with furry cat face and pants, a long tail, and a little red lacquered violin. A blue velvet vest with pearl buttons and an elegant 18th century loden frock coat trimmed with coral grosgrain along with a tricorn hat with coral colored feathers, set Kevin apart from his pals. Mark had to be a football player the minute he saw Uncle Charlie's old jersey and lace-up pants. He duded himself up in an old 1920s helmet and leather shoulder pads and insisted on carrying an old pigskin, as part of his get-up. Catching the absurd spirit of the dress rehearsal, Sancho selected an old one-piece striped woolen bathing suit, and stripped right there and then to try it on, to the hysterical laughter of the other guys.

On the night of the party, with Lamar at the wheel, Gaspar and Alex with their four pals, all dressed to the nines in their absurd costumes, pulled up to the school in the old woody. Excited to be invited to their first dance, they piled out of the car in a tangle of limbs, colorful costumes and laughter. Running up to the school gymnasium, they joined the stream of costumed revelers, shoving each other good-naturedly, while rearranging their finery, and laughing along the way.

Gaspar chose to be last in line, and followed behind his boisterous pals as they pushed their way through the crowd. That's when he saw Iilona standing to the side, as usual not participating in what was going on around her.

"Iilona, where have you been? I've been looking for you for weeks. What have you been up to? Come on, let's go to the party together." he coaxed her.

"I'm not going to the party, Gaspar. I've just come here to see all the kids in costume. By the way, I like what you're wearing the best" she complimented him. Could you wear it over to my house tomorrow to meet my mother and grandmother?"

"You want me to wear my Seminole Indian costume to meet your folks?" Gaspar asked incredulously. "*Tonight's* Halloween, Iilona, not *tomorrow*."

"Please wear it for me, and please come and visit."

"But, Iilona, I want to meet your family, but I don't know where the Seminole Spring is?" he argued, getting exasperated. "In fact, nobody I know, knows where it is."

"You own it, Gaspar. It's on the map, right here on Perdido Isle. I can't tell you how to get there. It's kind of remote. I just know how to get there by memory. I could lead you there tomorrow if you want, but then I'd have to meet you somewhere. Just look on the map, you'll find it. And don't forget, you have to come alone … promise."

"What time?" he asked, shortly, tired of playing games with her.

"Four o'clock," was her curt answer.

"Hey, Gaspar. Come on, get with it, hurry up!" his friends jeered from the gymnasium's doorway. Gaspar turned towards the commotion and signaled for his friends to shut up, but they kept up their cacophony. When he turned back, impatiently to speak to Iilona, she was gone. Gaspar spun around, but she was nowhere to be found. He ran back through the river of costumed friends, who were pressing forward towards the gym, but couldn't find Iilona anywhere. Finally giving up, he headed back towards the party, being carried along by the river of people, but Gaspar didn't see any of it. He was lost in thought about the weird girl who had so erratically entered his psyche. Finally catching up with his pals, Gaspar joined the party.

"What kept you?" Alex asked.

"I ran into Iilona," Gaspar explained.

"Which one is she?" Alex asked, looking around.

"She's not coming to the party. She's way too shy." Gaspar made excuses.

"I gotta meet this chick," Alex laughed. "She sounds really weird, Gasp."

"Keep your opinions to yourself, Al," Gaspar scolded his friend. "If you ever get to know her you'll understand that she's very special, a really nice girl," Gaspar informed him.

Just then June and some of her girlfriends came over to join the group. Gaspar noticed with amusement how all of his friends tensed up as the girls approached. Having had enough of their adolescent behavior, he decided to take action.

"June, isn't this our dance?" Gaspar asked, whisking her away before she could answer, leaving his speechless pals in the dust with their mouths hanging open. "This is gonna be fun, June."

"What?" June asked.

"To see exactly what Kevin, Alex, Mark, and Sancho do next. As for you and me, let's show them how it's done." Gaspar laughed, leading her onto the dance floor. When the D.J. turned up "Thriller," all the young couple could do was laugh as they took over the dance floor in imitation of the famous Michael Jackson video. All the cool kids at school had been practicing all week for this very moment and Gaspar and June were no exception.

Nothing could dim the glories of dancing with June, who was dressed as a lady from Louis XV's court, a costume she had made herself right down to her extravagantly jeweled white wig. Gaspar couldn't get out of his mind the incongruence of June in her Madame du Barry costume, showing off and dancing like crazy and

Iilona who he envisioned sulking somewhere outside in her beige shift with gingham trim, forever standing by the sideline, always … just watching. June's wig had been extravagantly curled and jeweled with rhinestones, all shiny white and lacquered. Iilona's long straight black hair was always parted down the middle and arranged in two long pigtails tied with limp red yarn. June's gown was icy blue taffeta, beribboned and bejeweled, and bouffant with dramatic panniers. Iilona's dress hung straight and shapeless from her shoulders. Drab was the only possible description that Gaspar could think of to describe her. June had painted her eyes with blue eye shadow and long black lashes. Iilona's eyes were beautiful, but they were big, huge, watery black cow-eyes, that never stopped staring. June's eyes, on the other hand, twinkled with playful laughter. What was it about that Seminole girl that had so captivated him, he wondered?

CHAPTER 15

THE SWAMP OF THE SPANISH VIRGINS

GASPAR DID NOT GO TO THE SEMINOLE SPRING THAT NEXT DAY AT FOUR O'CLOCK. IT'S NOT THAT HE didn't want to, it's just that he had no idea where the place was. Try as he may, he just hadn't been able to find out anything about a place on Perdido Isle called the Seminole Spring. Even Uncle Charlie had said that he'd never heard of the place, but there was something in the way he denied it's existence which made Gaspar wonder.

Instead of keeping his appointment, Gaspar decided to go sailing with Alex on the inland waterway between Perdido Isle and the mainland. Gaspar and Alex kept a little Sabot sailboat tied up at an old dock on a narrow inlet directly opposite La Rinconada. Gaspar appreciated that Uncle Charlie had purposefully built his house at the narrowest part of the hourglass-shaped island allowing easy access to both the Gulf and the inland waterway. Slipping the rope off of the pylon and hopping on board, the two pals peeled off their t-shirts and unfurled the sail. Now, the tiny sailboat with the two friends on board crept along the inlet between the tall reeds as it headed for the inland waterway.

"This is the life," Gaspar sang.

"Keep your eyes peeled for gators, Gasp," Alex insisted.

Before too long, the little ship which Gaspar had purchased used, from his friend and sailing instructor Craig Cadawalader, and christened *El Barquito*, was bucking the tiny white caps that the tradewinds had stirred up on the larger body of water.

"It's get-in kind-a choppy out here, Gasp," Alex complained.

"We're lucky we have the breeze at our backs, Al." I'm more worried about the trip back, to tell you the truth."

"We can tack back, Gasp. But we better leave enough time, or we'll miss dinner, and you know I never like to miss a meal."

"Tell me about it. If my mom cooked half as good as yours does, I'd be as big around as Chad," Gaspar referred to their friend and fellow club member.

"I'm just lucky I don't look like a hot air balloon … like Reginald." Alex quipped,

"It could be worse, Al. You could sound like Reginald, and you know what that sounds like."

"Yeah, it sounds like he has something stuck up his … "

"Hey," cried Gaspar from the prow. "Turn in there," he said pointing towards the island.

"Wha-da-ya see?" Alex asked, turning the rudder so that the boat crept towards the shore. "A gator?"

"I don't know, I thought I saw something … something interesting … pull into that inlet and let's take a look around."

"Gasp, Perdido Isle has so many inlets and swamps on this side, we could probably get lost for days tooling around inside there," Alex warned.

"Don't worry, Al. I just want to take a quick look around. I thought I saw something there. I can't explain it. Just keep going inland."

Soon the small craft entered a large lagoon, surrounded by tall reeds.

"Gator country!" Alex proclaimed. "Let's dock her here and look around," he suggested.

"Tell you what, Al. This isn't my favorite kind of terrain. Let's bring her in over there and see what happens," Gaspar pointed.

As the Sabot hit the sandy shore, Gaspar jumped out, and said, "wait for me here, Al … nature calls." Without waiting for an answer, he disappeared behind some tall reeds where he came upon a footpath and decided to follow it, at least for a short while. That's when he saw what he was looking for, what he thought he had seen earlier from the water.

"Iilona, Iilona, wait, it is I, Gaspar," he called, just like Mrs. Laker had taught him in English class, after the departing figure of a young girl with long braids.

Running after her, he finally caught up to where she was. She turned around to face him.

"Iilona, it is I, Gaspar. Why didn't you stop?" he asked the strange girl.

"Oh, Gaspar. It's good to see you. What are you doing so far out in the countryside … Um … so far from home?" she asked oddly.

"I was going to ask you the same question," Gaspar said, confused.

"But I'm not far from home. The Seminole Spring is just yonder. I come walking out here all the time."

"Iilona, I wanted to talk to you last night, but you disappeared. I haven't seen you at school in a long, long time. Is everything okay? Are you and your family all right?" Gaspar asked his friend, urgently, alarm in his voice.

"Oh, no … nothing's all right … not really. Iilona shook her head sadly. We have visitors now, and it has been very hard for us."

"Perhaps I could help you," Gaspar offered. "If there's anything you need … money, whatever, please just ask. You need to come back to school, Iilona. It's important."

"No, Gaspar. We don't need money. We just need to be left alone. I'm not interested in school. I'm only interested in keeping things as they are."

"What do you mean, Iilona? What are you talking about?" As usual Gaspar was getting frustrated with her again. "Why don't I go home with you right now and talk with your mother and grandmother. If you need help, I'm here for you, all you need do is ask," he promised.

"I do need your help, Gaspar, but not today. Today is not a good day. I will let you know when the time is right, I promise."

"Okay, Iilona. If you promise, then I'll leave you alone for now, but please don't hesitate to call me anytime if I can be of service. I really think you should come back to school, think about it, Iilona," Gaspar said. He wanted to put his arms around her for assurance, but she stepped back like a person who doesn't like to be touched. "Okay, then I'll see you soon, I hope, Iilona," he said taking a step backwards and waving goodbye.

Gaspar watched her turn around and proceed up the footpath. His inner voice said *follow her* but he didn't want to intrude, so he just walked backwards keeping her in his sight until she walked around a clump of pampas grass.

"Where have you been?" Alex asked, clearly put out by Gaspar's disappearing act.

"I had to take a leak, and then I thought I saw a gator so I went to look but it was only a heron moving around in the reeds."

"You were gonna tackle a gator by yourself, with your bare hands? Come on, Gasp, get real," Alex laughed.

"Tell you what, Al, let's head back out to the inland waterway. I want to leave a marker at the mouth of this inlet. I'd like to come back here and explore this place completely someday."

When they got to the end of the inlet, Gaspar tied his red t-shirt to an overhanging branch to mark the entrance to what he told Alex was a place where he'd like to build a house someday. Knowing his friend's desire to be an architect, Gaspar figured Alex would be fully occupied, quietly thinking for hours and hours about the future building project. Consequently, Gaspar wouldn't have to answer any more of his pal's nosey questions. Heading back onto the waterway, Gaspar suggested they return to La Rinconada. "It's gonna take an eternity to get home, Al, tacking back and forth against the current," Gaspar warned, "and we don't want to be out here in this bathtub after dark … that's for sure!"

"Don't you want to go a little further east, to look for other promising inlets?" Alex asked, hoping Gaspar would change his mind.

"No, Al, I want to get back. I think we should do some more investigating around here sooner than later, but not today. Besides … " Gaspar insisted, "I want to do some research in the library." Secretly he really wanted to learn a little bit more about this side of Perdido Isle and hoped some old surveys he had in the library would show him what he wanted to know.

Getting back to the ramshackle old dock near La Rinconada was tough sledding but finally by tacking back and forth for another hour and a half the boys eventually reached their destination. Picking up their bikes, they rode back across the road to the house, just in time to hear Alex's mom, Angela calling for him to come in to supper.

"See you tomorrow, Gasp," Alex sang as he split off from his pal and rode his bike through the arch into the stable yard.

Gaspar rode his red flyer over to the steps leading up to his front door and jumped off. When he came into the entrance hall he saw his mother at the top of the stairs waiting for him.

"Hi, dear," Elvira called. "Did you have a good time sailing? Did you find any gators? Are you ready for some dinner?" came the three questions to which she didn't expect any answers.

"Yes, no and yes," Gaspar answered her anyway. I'm going to the library to do some research, mom. When you're ready, just holler and I'll come runnin'!" Gaspar promised.

Entering the library, Gaspar took out a thick port-folio, bound in linen with a leather spine and leather corners. In the center of the cover was a leather plaque, and on the plaque embossed in gold were the words

Perdido Isle. He had seen the book before, and it had fascinated him, but it was also one of the most confusing documents he had ever perused. The book was a survey of all 500,000 of his acres including the island and all the land around it that was underwater. He had been told by Peter Cawthorne, in words that Gaspar could better understand, that basically he owned an area as large as his birthplace, the city of Los Angeles, not counting all the suburbs of course. When Peter had explained it to him that way, he understood instantly and completely the enormity of his inheritance. At last an adult who spoke plain English, was how Gaspar categorized Peter that day.

Turning the pages of the folio he found a table of contents, which basically meant nothing to him. Listed there was Calaluna and Llojeta, as well as various place names like Smuggler's Cove, La Rinconada and other names that he had never heard spoken, but would like to match up with places he had visited on his bike, or in the car with Lamar, or like today, sailing in the Sabot.

"Seminole Spring, Seminole Spring, Seminole Spring ... " he whispered under his breath ... there it was, the Seminole Spring, page 468. Gaspar turned a huge handful of pages over and then little by little made his way backwards to page 465, 466, 469, 470 ... Wait a minute, page 467 and 468 were missing. *"Blubbering, blue blistering barnacles,"* he Captain Haddocked. "Someone's stolen my map!"

Not ready to give up, he went back to the main map that showed the entire above-water part of the island, in miniature. He tried to figure out where he and Alex had been that afternoon. Quickly he grabbed the huge horn-handled magnifying glass off Uncle Charlie's desk and started going over the map, inch by inch, reading all the names of all the different inlets, bays and outcroppings. He thought he saw the place where Iilona had caught his attention this afternoon. It was called *Swamp of the Spanish Virgins*, if he was looking at the right place on the correct map. The map said that the inlet was called *Spanish Creek*, and the large pond at its far end was called *Lago Maldonado*.

Turning more pages in the massive folio, he thought he'd found the place where he'd seen Iilona earlier. Tracing his finger inland from the waterway, he found what he was looking for ... THE SEMINOLE SPRING. Gaspar's pulse raced and a chill shuddered down his body before he flushed, white hot. His excitement in finally finding some reference to where Iilona lived, for whatever reason, made his blood run simultaneously, hot and then cold.

Taking out his phone, he snapped a picture of the map, and then another, zeroing in on the name place. Thinking twice, he flipped the pages back to the map which identified Spanish Creek, and snapped that too. Replacing the book where he'd found it, he raced up the library's spiral staircase and through the secret panel which lead into his amazing bedroom, the Captain's Cabin, which Uncle Charlie had cleverly built to look like the captain's cabin on a Spanish galleon. From his bedroom he crossed through his lapis lazuli bathroom and stepped through the connecting door leading into the former blue bedroom, which he had recently converted into his office. There he downloaded the two photographs he'd just snapped, blew them up and printed them out in triplicate.

CHAPTER 16

ANOTHER ROBBERY

Aᴠᴛᴇʀ sᴄʜᴏᴏʟ ᴛʜᴇ ᴠᴏʟʟᴏᴡɪɴɢ Fʀɪᴅᴀʏ, Gᴀsᴘᴀʀ ᴀɴᴅ Aʟᴇx sᴛᴏᴘᴘᴇᴅ ʙʏ Pᴇᴛᴇʀ Cᴀᴡᴛʜᴏʀɴᴇ's ᴏꜰꜰɪᴄᴇ ᴛᴏ hang out and hear the scuttlebutt around town from Peter's cool college intern, Brewster Wharton. When they walked in the door, they found Peter, Brewster and Mrs. Crabtree, Peter's faithful confidential secretary talking animatedly.

"Hey, guys. Hello, Mrs. Crabtree," Gaspar called out as he and Alex breezed into the office. "What's up?"

"Hello, Gaspar," Peter greeted the two boys. "Hi, Alex. Come on in."

"There's been another robbery this morning," Brewster informed them by way of greeting.

"No! What happened this morning … tell us about it?" Gaspar begged, wide-eyed.

"Old lady Manville was burgled this morning while she was out at the hairdressers," Peter informed him.

"Did they get away with a lot of loot?"

"Plenty. The old gal had one of the best known collections of pink diamonds in the world," Peter informed him.

"Have the cops got any better leads on the robbers this time?" Gaspar asked breathlessly.

"Naw, the culprits seem to have disappeared into thin air … as usual," Brewster jumped in.

"I'm glad we're not living in Llojeta. That town must be in lockdown mode at this point," whispered Mrs. Crabtree demurely.

"Yeah, Mrs. Crabtree. I've got an extra guard at La Rinconada, too." Gaspar said.

"Have you been threatened?" Mrs. Crabtree seemed horrified.

"Naw, Mrs. Crabtree." Gaspar lied, catching Peter's eye. "Better safe than sorry."

"What are you boys up to this afternoon?" Peter asked.

"We just wanted to stop by and say hi, but now I think I'll head down to headquarters and talk with Captain Morgan. I'd like to learn more about those pink diamonds," Gaspar stated.

• • •

Entering the police captain's office, Gaspar and Alex were greeted with enthusiasm.

"Gaspar, just the man I wanted to see." Captain Morgan stood up to welcome the boys. "Hello, Alex. Have you brought me news? What more have you to tell me about Señora Martinez de Gozz spectacular jeweled dagger?"

To Gaspar's amusement, Alex looked at the police chief totally befuddled, before Gaspar jumped in and let him off the hook. "I've gone over it and over it in my head, Captain Morgan. Do you have time to listen to my theory? The only thing I can come up with is a supposition."

"Go ahead, Gaspar, I'm all ears," the chief implored his young friend, as he sat back down in his big leather desk chair.

"Yeah, Gasp. Go ahead, Captain Morgan and I are all ears." Alex sat down and crossed his arms over his chest, waiting to hear Gaspar's whopper.

"Well, the way I see it … it's like this, captain. Four guys pile out of a royal blue sedan and go up to the Ambassador Suite and rob the old Argentinean lady. Four different guys wearing similar clothes leave via the service entrance. Those guys dump the blue sedan somewhere in the jungle. You have found and impounded a blue sedan, haven't you?"

"Yes, Gaspar, but that is top secret police information." Captain Morgan was indignant.

"Anyway, captain, it doesn't matter. The four men and the driver all got into various other cars which they'd stationed somewhere along the road earlier in the day. Some took off in pairs, some alone, some drove to Calaluna, some back into Llojeta, and maybe some even drove over to the mainland. If you had caught them, which you didn't, you would have discovered that the jewels weren't on them nor were their fingerprints anywhere near the Ambassador Suite. In fact, captain, I think that the jewels are still in the hotel. One of those other four men, the men who actually did the robbery, handed the jewels over to someone, possibly of German origin, who had previously checked into the hotel. The four guys who got out of that car, probably never even entered Señora de Gozz's room. If you could take fingerprints of the four guys who entered and the four guys who left, I bet they would not match up to any fingerprints in the Ambassador Suite. That's all I have to say. If I were you, I'd be looking for a very rich German, possibly a man with a yacht, who hopefully hasn't checked out yet. That's where you'll find the loot. Forget about the four men and the driver who got away. They probably were paid to do just that, walk out the door and switch cars. They probably had no idea that a crime was being committed while they were walking down the hall. Same goes for the four dupes who came in through the service entrance. There are four other guys, possibly posing as part of a convention or as a group of happy fishermen, or businessmen with their wives. They are the ones who tied up the Señora and her maid. They're the ones who opened the safe and took the stuff, but they are all just decoration. They dropped the loot off, possibly in an adjoining suite, or maybe one of those four was the big boss himself and the others didn't even know it. All he had to do was stride down the hall and let himself into his own room, while the other five disappeared into the scene of the crowded hotel."

"Gaspar, you amaze me. Do you really think all of that is possible?" the captain asked.

"Yeah, Gasp … you amaze me too." Alex threw in, wide-eyed.

"I can practically guarantee it," Gaspar bragged.

"What about your mother's jewels?" the captain wondered.

"Yeah, Gasp … *What!*" Alex was back to being befuddled again.

"Those were just the icing on the cake. The big prize was the jeweled dagger, all the rest of the robberies are the MacGuffin.

"The MacGuffin, what's a MacGuffin?" Captain Morgan puzzled.

"Yeah, what's a McMuffin?" Alex was really getting balled up.

"The red herring, the diversion, the slight of hand." Gaspar expounded. "Haven't either of you ever seen an Alfred Hitchcock movie? None of it means anything to the big boss as long as he has the jeweled dagger. That's the prize. I can assure you. Anyway, I've got a feeling they're hiding out in a place where nobody on this island would ever consider looking. A place that even the old-timers have forgotten," Gaspar mused. "I'll have a little more information on that gang shortly, captain. The one you want however, the real prize … is the German king pin. I can't put my finger on it, but it's really the dagger they were after. The diamonds were small potatoes in comparison, wait and see."

Alex was now sitting in stunned silence while his pal laid out his hair-brained theories on a multi-million dollar heist to none other than the chief of police. After they left the office, Alex found his voice again. "What the *huggermugger*, Gaspar? Since when have you become the Hercule Poirot of Perdido Isle, and what's this about you mother's jewels. Have you been holding out on me, *bro*?"

"Don't get your knickers in a twist, Al," Gaspar chided him. "Someone broke in to La Rinconada and took some of my mom's costume jewelry. No big deal, but that's why I've doubled the guard. Better safe than sorry, you know," he shrugged off Alex's look of disbelief.

"What have you got in mind now? Can I help you find the robbers, or do you want to hog all the glory for yourself?" Alex showed his hurt feelings.

"Don't get all *fuzzy-wuzzy on me, you foul-anchored freshwater pirate*, of course you're gonna help me. Here's what I want to do … "

• • •

The next morning Gaspar and Alex left La Rinconada together, but they took separate routes to reach the same destination. Gaspar took his red flyer and headed down the road towards Llojeta. Alex took his old bike and headed across the road for the boat dock and the Sabot. Gaspar had instructed his pal to sail back to the inlet where he had tied his red t-shirt the other day. When he got there he was to sail up the inlet all the way to the end, then follow the foot path inland towards the Seminole Spring. Gaspar had given Alex one of his maps, and he'd purposely left the other on the desk in The Captain's Cabin, his bedroom at La Rinconada. The third map he'd printed out was folded into a neat square and placed in the pocket of his jeans. Gaspar would approach the Seminole Spring from the land side, via bicycle and Alex would approach by water. The plan was to meet up in the middle, while keeping a close eye out for any suspicious characters. If Gaspar's hunch was correct, he hoped to discover the secret hideout being used by the jewel thieves.

Gaspar was the first on the scene, and left his bike in the brush by the side of an old Indian footpath. He was pushing through some tall grass when he came upon Iilona, standing with her back to him, looking out over a sparkling pond.

"Iilona, it is I, Gaspar," he whispered, not wanting to startle her, while thinking how proud his favorite teacher, Mrs. Laker, would be of his perfect English.

"Shhh, Gaspar," the girl cautioned, waving her hand in a downward position, without bothering to turn around.

"What is it, Iilona?" Gaspar whispered, coming up close behind her. He was so close that he thought he detected the scent of cut grass in her hair, but suddenly realized that the girl actually had no scent … none at all. "Iilona, what are you doing?" As usual, he was starting to get frustrated with her again.

"You want to find the robbers, don't you," she whispered matter-of-factly.

"Yes, of course I do. How'd you know?"

"Then keep quiet, and follow me," she said with a complete lack of emotion.

"Let me call Alex," Gaspar begged.

"No," was her quick response. "Just follow me!"

Gaspar followed the girl, around the pond, deep into a mangrove swamp. Continuing along what could only have been ancient Indian trails, they passed through a high clump of cattails and peered around and through a massive display of mondo grass. What Gaspar saw there took his breath away. In all of his wonderings on Perdido Isle he'd never seen such a beautiful, idyllic natural landscape. There, laid out in front of them was the most beautiful clear lake of still water, surrounded by mature trees of many varieties, flowering shrubs, and moss-covered stone outcroppings. Besides the lake's impressive flora and fauna, the marine life Gaspar saw was vast and varied. Large silver and goldfish with iridescent scales swam close to the lake's surface, while exotic birds walked on tall legs in the shallow waters near the water's edge. Ducks, geese and swans floated on the surface amidst flowering lily pads, as toads croaked a mighty chorus. No end of wild birds and iridescent insects jeweled the air. Peacocks strutted along the banks or called out from perches high up in the moss-covered trees. Gaspar wouldn't doubt that at least 100 different species of mammals might live in this enchanted bio-climate. He saw deer, possum, peccaries and wouldn't be surprised if there were even monkeys, mountain lions and jaguars hiding somewhere in the undergrowth, along with gators too. Farther along he could see an inlet, which was part of a coral reef, complete with teaming tide pools surrounded by more fresh and saltwater lagoons, as well as mangroves, sand dunes and endless wetlands.

As if she were reading his mind, Iilona whispered, "there used to be monkeys here too, but they disappeared after hurricane Roxanne. The Seminole Spring is also home to an amazing diversity of birds, both permanent and migratory, which we have spotted including herons, egrets, pelicans and cranes. I've counted at least 350 species myself, but my grandmother is the real bird-watcher in the family."

"So this is the Seminole Spring," Gaspar exhaled, looking around him.

To his delight, an island in the middle of the lake could be reached via a causeway from the opposite shore. The island held a three-story Queen Anne cottage with deep overhanging balconies and a tall observation tower built in stages like a Chinese pagoda. The delightful Gingerbread-Victorian house was painted white with bright red trim, and although it was weathered and slightly falling down, it held an alluring mixture of both charm and mystery which appealed to Gaspar's aesthetic sensibilities, as well as his spirit of adventure.

"Yes, Gaspar, this is the Seminole Spring and that is my home."

"It's like something out of a fairy tale, you know, an *enchanted* place," Gaspar tried to wrap his head around it.

"In a way, it is enchanted, Gaspar. This is where I have lived with my grandmother and my mother for many, many years. This is what I have wanted to show you. But now that you're here, it's not a good time to pay a social call."

"Why not? There's no time like the present," Gaspar smiled broadly, stepping forward.

"No wait, you must stay hidden. It's not safe." She hissed at him under her breath.

"Not safe, don't be ridiculous, Iilona. What do you mean, not safe?"

Suddenly Gaspar saw movement on the other side of the lake. A surly-looking giant of a man was leaving Iilona's house. He didn't look left or right but strode directly towards the road, which was a long way off. Gaspar figured, if his hunch was right and the stranger was one of the jewel gang, they'd be using another, probably more direct route than the one Gaspar had just taken to come in. Whatever the answer, the man's presence caused Gaspar's stomach to tighten and the hair on the back of his neck to stand up.

Gaspar pulled himself together, gulped and whispered, "Who is that man, Iilona? Is he one of the jewel thieves?"

"Yes, Gaspar. He is evil."

"Is the coast clear now? Can we go inside?" he asked, shaking a shiver down his spine.

"No, he's going out now, but there are still three men inside the house. There is also a fifth man, the boss man, but he's out in the speedboat."

"So they have a speedboat ... " Gaspar mused, "Have they hidden the loot in there?"

"Yes, Gaspar. It is hidden inside the house."

"I need to get inside, Iilona." Gaspar took out his cell phone and dialed Alex. "But before I do, I'm going to need some back-up."

"Hello," Alex answered in an irritated voice.

"What's wrong? Gaspar could barely speak, his heart pounded so excitedly in his throat.

"Gasp, I've never left the dock. Someone's stolen the Sabot. I've already called Sergeant O'Malley to report the robbery." Alex cried anxiously.

"Listen, Al, better yet, call Lieutenant Jacobson at the Calaluna Coast Guard Station and ask him to pick you up. Also call Peter and tell him to get on board too. You lead them to the mouth of the inlet, along with a squad of policemen. Tell Lieutenant Jacobson to block the exit to The Swamp of the Spanish Maidens, and you lead them in the back way. Make sure Peter is with you. Al … the jewel thieves are here! I've found their hideout! You gotta come quick! I'll call Captain Morgan and ask him to bring a squad on board with you. I'll also ask him to get Sergeant O'Malley to bring in another squad from the road. We need to surprise these jokers *right now!*" Gaspar rang off.

Next he speed-dialed Captain Morgan, who picked up on the first ring. "Captain, Gaspar Brown here. I have your robbers."

"What robbers?"

"*The jewel thieves!* They're hiding out at the Seminole Spring."

"Is that a health spa?"

"No, it's not a health spa, it's a place, right here on Perdido Isle. Listen, captain, you gotta get over here right away. I've got Alex and Lieutenant Jacobson bottling up the way out via The Swamp of the Spanish Virgins. You should send a squad over to the coast guard right now so they can hitch a ride with them. Meanwhile, on your way out here via the Llojeta Road, stop off at La Rinconada and find a Xerox of a map I left on my desk in the captain's cabin."

"What's that?"

"That's my bedroom … anyhow, the map will show you how to get to The Seminole Spring … and captain, hurry … I'm all alone here, and there's five of them!" Gaspar pressed *end* and rang off.

"Let's go, Iilona."

"You can't go in there."

"I want to secure the loot, the evidence."

"You better wait for your friends." Iilona cautioned wisely.

"By the way, Iilona, while we're waiting for the cavalry … you should have called the police a long time ago." Gaspar chided her.

"Me, call the police?" Iilona looked stupefied. "But we have no phone, Gaspar."

"But Iilona, if they let you out, if they weren't holding you hostage … you should have gone to the police, or something. I guess what I'm saying is … you should have told me about this situation sooner," Gaspar said, exasperated, or as Alex would have said, ex-*gasper*-ated.

"I couldn't do that. I knew you would come. Besides, you need to do whatever you need to do, Gaspar. I know you've had previous experience with this kind of thing. Besides, I'm just not capable, not with something like this." Iilona's rantings made no sense to him, but he had more important things on his mind just now than to try and figure out his strange friend's foibles.

"How many men are still inside, Iilona?"

"Right now, only three." A gruff voice snarled behind him.

Gaspar whirled around, fearing the worst. The tall gruff man stood over him menacingly. Now he knew where the guy he saw leaving the house had gone to. Gaspar turned to warn Iilona to run, but she was already gone. Turning back to face the intruder he saw the man's huge hand bearing down on him, before he could say a word or try to get away, Gaspar's world went black.

When Gaspar woke up, he found himself tied up and tossed in the back of a speeding motorboat. His head throbbed, and the ropes that tied his wrists behind his back cut into his skin, as he bounced up and down on the hard deck of the small craft. His ankles also throbbed from the restraints that had been placed there. He was a helpless captive. Through narrowed-eyes, he could see that the driver was the giant who'd clobbered him. There was also another man onboard who sat in the seat behind him, but he couldn't see him. He only knew he was there because he could hear him talking very excitedly with a very thick German accent, while his feet kicked Gaspar's backside, annoyingly keeping tempo with his guttural lingo. Gaspar wondered if the mystery man was the fifth member of the gang or perhaps even … the big boss?

• • •

"There's an inlet just up ahead that's called The Swamp of the Spanish Virgins, lieutenant. If you leave us off just up stream, there's a footpath that will take us directly to the Seminole Spring where Gaspar has his eyes on the robbers," Alex explained to Lieutenant Carl Jacobson of the coast guard, as the cruiser *Orion* chugged up the inland waterway. It's a large area, so I think Gaspar's idea of bringing in reinforcements from land and sea is a good one."

"Let me see the map, please," Lieutenant Jacobson asked, taking the Xerox from Alex's hand.

Just as *Orion* entered the inlet leading to The Swamp of the Spanish Virgins, a swift lime green motorboat raced around a bend heading straight for the larger craft. Seeing the speedboat approaching, the lieutenant blew the horn to warn the craft to slow down, while simultaneously turning the wheel causing the much larger *Orion* to completely block the smaller boat's exit out into the inland waterway. The pilot of the sleek Chris Craft had only one option. He threw his motor into reverse, while turning the wheel sharply to the left, causing his boat to skid sideways before thumping into the coast guard cruiser broadside amidst a wave of white foam and spray. The small boat splashed to a halt tossing its occupants, including Gaspar, sideways across its deck. A crowd of uniformed officers watched from the rail of

Orion. When Alex saw who was tied up in the speedboat, he let out a mighty roar.

"Gaspar, they've got Gaspar! Lieutenant Jacobson, that's Gaspar trussed up back there," Alex shouted to all who would listen.

Lieutenant Jacobson grabbed a megaphone and hollered down to the stunned driver of the speedboat and his well-dressed passenger. "This is the United States Coast Guard. You are under arrest. Place your hands on your heads where we can see them. We have you covered, there is no escape. Surrender your weapons and my men will escort you on board peaceably."

With that, five guardsmen boarded the small craft placing the driver and his henchman in handcuffs, while freeing Gaspar from his bonds.

Gaspar had been stunned by the impact of the smaller boat against the cruiser, but he was able to stand. Once he regained his balance, he smiled wanly up at his friends and called to them in a shaky voice. "Lieutenant, Peter, Al, thanks for coming to the rescue … you're not a minute too soon." He chuckled weakly, "just in the nick of time." That's when he noticed the man who had been sitting behind him, being hustled on board the cruiser. He was the same dude that had been eyeing him at Karen's Café the other day. Karen mentioned his German accent at the time. Gaspar wondered if he might be the kingpin?

Once onboard *Orion*, Gaspar was able to inform the coast guard and the police squad, headed by Captain

Morgan himself, of the situation up ahead. Taking the map from Lieutenant Jacobson's hands, Gaspar was able to show his saviors the lay of the land. "Here is where I was hit on the head and kidnapped," Gaspar said, pointing out a spot on the map. "You'll probably find my red flyer in the bushes somewhere over here," he pointed to the spot where he thought he'd left his bicycle. "Sergeant O'Malley and his men should be coming in from the road here, and we can enter the area from the water over here. See this island in the middle of the lake? There's an old house on it, and that is where you'll find the thieves and the loot," Gaspar insisted.

"How do you know that, Gasp?" Peter asked.

"Because my friend lives there and she told me that the robbers had taken over the house. Right after, that's when I was clobbered by that *hairy-headed highwayman!*" he said pointing to the criminal who had been driving the speedboat, but who now sat sheepishly on deck holding his head in his massive handcuffed hands.

"Okay, Gaspar, let's go and see. If nothing else, at least we can reclaim your lost bike," Captain Morgan seemed doubtful that the end of the case was going to really be that easy.

Lieutenant Jacobson called out his orders, and *Orion* with Peter, Gaspar, Alex, Felix and six uniformed policemen, as well as a full contingent of coast guardsmen, headed up the inland waterway into The Swamp of the Spanish Virgins. When they got there, Gaspar waved to his pal Lieutenant Jacobson, who was on the bridge to pull into the sand along the right side of the inlet. It was almost the same spot where Gaspar had pretended to Al that he had to take a leak, just the other day.

"This is it," Gaspar proclaimed, as he jumped ship, "follow me."

Quickly he led them along the footpath where he had run into Iilona the other day, and continued past the clump of high bushes that she had previously disappeared behind. Gaspar slowed his pace, and like an Indian scout stooped low and crept along the winding path, knowing that any minute now the Seminole Spring would appear … like magic. As they got closer to their goal, the landscape changed dramatically, becoming even more lush, more verdant, more tropical, variegated and flowered. Colorful birds began to swirl in the sky, while iridescent insects fluttered and buzzed all around them. Leading the authorities through a clump of flowering hibiscus … suddenly … there it was, peeking out between two big-eared elephant plants … the Seminole Spring. Gaspar motioned with his hands for everyone to slow down, and put his fingers to his lips so that they would remain silent.

Turning towards Captain Morgan, he whispered, "This is it, captain. Do you think your reinforcements are near? That is the old house, he said pointing off to the left. There is a spit of land connecting the island to terra firma over there, on the opposite side of where we are. Perhaps we should circle the pond clockwise from here, and get over to the house. It's the only way on or off that little island, so if they're inside we can have a standoff, right there," Gaspar suggested.

Captain Morgan nodded his agreement and called Sergeant O'Malley, who was coming in from the road with his reinforcements, to make sure they were all on the same page. "The crooks must have a car near here, so make sure the entrance from the road is blocked and guarded," he ordered O'Malley, before pressing *end*.

"Or maybe they only come and go by speedboat," Gaspar suggested.

"With *Orion* blocking the inlet, I'd say we've covered any escape by water pretty thoroughly," Captain Morgan boasted.

With thick tropical foliage hiding their advance, the group crept slowly around the edge of the pond. More than once they came upon deer and other animals who did not scamper away, but held their ground completely unafraid of the human invasion. Reaching the causeway that led to the small island, Captain Morgan called O'Malley again and ordered a diversion be created on the opposite shore from where they were now positioned. The pond, which was now entirely encircled, soon echoed with the sound of gunshots from the opposite shore. Three men came running out of the Queen Anne cottage to see what was going on and raced around the covered porch, which encircled the house on all four sides. When the crooks were clear on the other side of the house, Captain Morgan gave the signal for his group to cross the bridge and take over. Hearing the clatter, the criminals discovered too late that they'd been tricked into showing themselves. They were now hemmed in by uniformed officers standing on the covered porch, as well as more coppers, who had stepped forward, guns drawn, lining the water's edge. There was no escape. Gaspar imagined that they must also have been more surprised than pleased to see that amongst them was the boy billionaire himself, who had turned up like a bad penny.

While the official business of the capture took place, Gaspar quickly extricated himself from the others and stepped inside the old house. What he found there was a revelation. It was a mess. Fully-furnished, but falling down. The wallpaper hung off the walls in long strips. The plaster ceilings were riddled with huge holes where massive chunks had fallen down, exposing the crude lath underneath. Old kerosene lamp chandeliers hung loosely from fancy gilded plaster medallions set into the ceiling. Here and there, cut crystals twinkled in the late afternoon sun. Parquet floors with intricate inlaid patterns had buckled and popped up. Old marble fireplaces, probably imported from France at the turn of the century, sat cold and cracked, not having seen a fire burned in them for decades. Lace curtains and fancy scalloped draperies hung, rotted and split, at the windows, whose colored panes were now cracked and in some instances entirely missing. Dry, dusty and faded carpets, strewn with patterns of roses and garlands of leaves, covered the floors. There were even vases with the decomposed remains of fancy floral arrangements, old lace doilies and many porcelain knick-knacks strewn here and there on shelves in dusty vitrines, and across tabletops.

Climbing up the rickety stairs, he found more of the same … bedrooms with suites of old furniture and rotting linens. He couldn't believe it … at the end of the hall was a bathroom with indoor plumbing, old and dated and charming in its incongruity. Without too much trouble he found the stairs leading up into the tower. Slowly, feeling each tread, lest his mere ninety pound frame crash through the rotting timbers, he made it to the top, and through a trap door to the open air observation platform. That's where he found Iilona, her mother, and her grandmother.

"Iilona, it is I, Gaspar," he said by way of greeting.

The three strangely dressed women turned around and smiled at him.

"Gaspar, this is my mother and my grandmother. They have been wanting to meet you," she said.

"How do you do," Gaspar bowed slightly, as they hadn't extended their hands. He thought bowing might be the approved Seminole way of greeting strangers.

"We've been watching the activity on The Swamp of the Spanish Virgins," Iilona explained. "We cheered when the coast guard picked up your kidnapper and his ugly green boat too."

"You should have been there, Iilona. It was crazy," Gaspar filled her in. "The police have just captured the rest of the gang," Gaspar told them, although he figured that they'd been watching the entire show from their box seats up in the tower.

"That's good. We counted on you to help us get those evil men out of here, Gaspar," Iilona said.

"And I'm counting on you to tell me where the stolen loot is," Gaspar insisted.

"They hid it in the old icebox in the kitchen," Iilona said, matter-of-factly.

"Listen, Iilona, I've got to go downstairs and conclude this business. Will you and your mother and grandmother wait for me here while I go downstairs to show the police captain the loot. I need to give him the sparklers right away. Please promise that you'll wait for me. I'll be right back."

Iilona's only answer was to smile and shake her head in the affirmative.

With that promise, Gaspar scampered through the trap door and down the back servants' stairs, which lead directly to the old-fashioned kitchen. Once there, he opened the latch on the door of the old icebox and found a canvas bag inside. Opening it he discovered all the loot … not the least of which was a magnificent jeweled dagger. Grabbing the jeweled object, Gaspar looked at it from every angle, then proceeded to try and twist the large ruby which covered the entire butt of the handle, hoping that it would open and reveal a secret compartment. When it wouldn't budge, he decided that his hunch must have been wrong. Then he felt one of the cabochon stones he was fingering push inward, and instantly the ruby butt sprang open on an invisible gold hinge. *Eureka, I've found it.* He patted himself on the back. Hitting the open butt against his upturned palm he felt something inside slide forward. Using his pinky he was able to extricate a tightly rolled-up document written on thin onion skin paper, which he placed in his jean's pocket without even looking at it. Satisfied that the butt of the dagger was now empty, he pushed the ruby cover back in place and heard the mechanism that secured it, snap closed. Quickly he replaced the dagger into the canvas bag and walked out, through the dining room and into the front hall where Alex, Peter and Captain Morgan were looking around in awe.

"Here's the loot, captain," Gaspar called, as he entered the entrance hall. "Check it out. I think it's all here including my mother's pieces, and Señora de Gozz's jeweled dagger too.

"Well done, Gaspar. Thank you, my friend, for solving this mystery and for breaking the ring of robbers." Captain Morgan thumped Gaspar on the back with one of his huge paws, nearly knocking the boy off his feet.

All here and all accounted for," smiled Captain Morgan, looking inside the bag.

"They had it hidden in the old icebox in the kitchen, all placed just like this, using this convenient old canvas bag," Gaspar marveled.

"How'd you ever find it? How'd you know where to look?" Peter asked, with just a hint of suspicion in his voice.

"I just figured, where else would you keep *hot ice until it cools off* if you were a bunch of *jabbernowled kleptomaniacs* like these guys were, *but in an icebox*," Gaspar quipped.

"Gaspar, where do you come up with words like *jabbernowled kleptomaniacs*?" Peter exclaimed, smiling broadly, while shaking his head in approval.

"I know, Peter, it's not quite a Captain Haddock curse. But it will do in a pinch," Gaspar joked.

"Gaspar, have you always known about this place?" Peter asked in disbelief.

"No, Peter. My friend from school lives here with her folks." Gaspar explained. "Remember how I've been asking everyone I know about the Seminole Spring? Well this is it!"

"Gaspar, if they are tenants of yours I don't think they're paying any rent." Peter insisted.

"Yeah, Peter, I know. I appreciate that you're always looking out for my best interests, but the family were good friends of my great uncle. I think he gave them this place *gratis*, in perpetuity. We'll have to ask Margaret Stewart to look for those agreement papers." Gaspar lied.

"I'd like to meet these friends of yours, Gasp." Peter obviously didn't believe him.

"Yeah, Peter. They must have gone out of town or something. They're not here. I was just looking for them. I guess the crooks found an empty house, and just took it over. Look at the mess they made of it." Gaspar hoped he was going to get away with his far-fetched story.

"Well, Gasp, it's getting late and I think we should all head home now," Peter suggested.

"Listen, you guys, I've been through a lot today. I wonder if you'd do me a favor and leave me here, alone, just for a little while. When you get back to La Rinconada, send Lamar to get me. And Al, maybe you'd come with him, and bring some cookies … okay," he begged them to understand.

CHAPTER 17

A SEMINOLE BRAVE

AFTER EVERYONE HAD LEFT, GASPAR ENTERED THE DRAWING ROOM AND CAME FACE TO FACE WITH Iilona's family. The two ladies were sitting peacefully in their decrepit drawing room as if they were waiting for someone to drop by for a cream tea. Iilona, who was standing when he came into the room, now sat down next to her grandmother, and Gaspar sat down across from them. Not wanting to waste a precious minute, Gaspar started in with his game of 53 questions.

"Iilona, can you explain all of this to me, please, once and for all. What's going on here?" he asked.

"Gaspar, it is a long story. I will tell it to you. Please be patient, it's been a long time since we have told anyone this tale. The Seminole Spring is an *enchanted* place. It was the domain of our family and our people

171

for hundreds of years. This land, Perdido Isle has passed from one generation of Seminoles to the other, until the Spanish came and took it from us. My forefathers were chiefs. My grandmother, my mother, and even I, we are all Seminole princesses. This sacred spring, this entire place was important to my people, and it was passed from father to son from time immemorial. At some point in the early 19th century, a spell was placed over this spring by a powerful medicine man. It was his intention that the land should always remain Seminole, and that it should only pass from father to son. My grandmother is pure Seminole, and my mother was an only child. My mother married my father, also a pure bred Seminole, and I am her only daughter. So you see, for three generations my family has not produced a son and until a son, an heir, comes forward … we cannot leave this place. My grandmother was born in 1850, my mother was born in 1870 and I was born in 1890."

Gaspar felt like the floor had just fallen out from under his chair, as he sat speechless listening to this extraordinary tale.

"I fell in love with your Uncle Charlie, and he built me this house in 1910 as a wedding present. Before we could wed, while he was away in Europe, my grandmother, my mother and I were killed … washed out to sea in the hurricane that struck the gulf that year. When your Uncle Charlie returned from Europe, we were dead, and this house was severely damaged. He never returned here, and as you can see, we never left."

"You mean, you are ghosts?" Gaspar stuttered.

"Phantoms," Iilona whispered.

Gaspar looked around at the three ladies, and it all became so clear and made so much sense. The house, the way they were dressed, their hopelessness. "I understand," he whispered back. "How can I help you?" he asked.

"My grandmother, my mother and I want to adopt you, as a Seminole brave. That way the land will be truly yours, not just in deed, since your great-great uncle purchased it legally, so many years ago. As a Seminole brave it will also be spiritually yours, like a sacred trust. We feel you have been sent to us for this reason, and that you will honor the beauty and purity of *The Seminole Spring* as long as you live. If you will agree to undertake this sacred trust for us, we will be released from the enchantment and be free to move on. Please, Gaspar, help set us free," Iilona begged him.

"Iilona, you know I will. But I must know the spring's boundaries."

"That is easy, Gaspar. You will know the boundaries, just by walking north, south, east and west from the banks of the spring. Your inner voice, your natural instincts will tell you when you have left the area of enchantment."

"Then I make a solemn promise to you three ladies," Gaspar said, standing up. "I, Gaspar Brown, a Seminole brave will from this day forward protect the Seminole

Spring in perpetuity," he vowed, crossing his heart, while hoping to die.

The three phantom ladies stood up as one, and smiled broadly as they slowly disappeared right before his very eyes.

Gaspar sat back down on the rickety old chair, stunned. What could possibly happen to him next that could beat that. Getting up again, he went outside to get some air and found a seat in a basket chair on the porch. When he looked up, there was Uncle Charlie perched on the balcony railing, looking out over the water.

"It certainly is a beautiful spot, Gaspar," the old ghost said. "So you met Iilona ... I'm glad. She was the great love of my life, my big heartbreak," he told Gaspar sadly.

"Uncle, did I do the right thing? Will I be able to fulfill my promise?" Gaspar wondered.

"More than I have, Gasp." He had never seen Uncle Charlie so morose. "I protected it through neglect, and the spell took care of the rest. Now that a real Seminole brave is in possession of the property, the legend will live on. The sacred land will remain pure, and the ladies, and my darling Iilona will be happy at last."

"You never saw her again, uncle?" Gaspar needed to know.

"No, I didn't have the heart. She never appeared to me, not in the way she did to you. Even after I died, I couldn't bear the idea of seeing her again. Better to let bygones be bygones, too much water under the bridge. You know all the old sayings, Gasp."

"Love sounds really complicated, uncle. I'm not so sure I'm ready to grow up and go through heartbreak like you have," Gaspar said wisely.

"Well, Gasp, if only you had a choice. But you don't, you see. Love comes to you when you least expect it, and it can be taken away from you just as fast. When it comes, grab it, you won't regret it. Better to be loved once than not at all. You'll see. So what are your plans for the Seminole Spring? Knowing the way you operate, I'm sure you've already formulated a plan!"

"Well, uncle, I've only given it two minutes of thought. First I'll make it a nature preserve, a wildlife conservancy and botanical garden. I'll ask June and her girls to care of it. Of course, uncle, you know I want to restore this house, exactly the way it was planned … and I do mean,,, exactly!"

"You'll find all the plans for it in the library. Margaret Stewart has probably come across them by now. You'll find a folio of all the furniture, china, crystal, even the wallpapers, fabrics and carpet samples. It's a big box, you'll see. That was always one of my faults. I just never threw anything away." Uncle Charlie chuckled with a sigh.

"Let's get out-a here, Uncle Charlie. Lamar is coming to pick me up, and I may as well be waiting for him by the road, and you can help me find my red flyer too," Gaspar suggested, as they walked together back towards the road.

That night, after a hearty dinner with his mom, Peter and Alex, Gaspar went straight up to his room, exhausted. It was while he was undressing for the night that he found the curled up parchment that he'd extracted from the jeweled dagger, in his jeans' pocket. Gaspar was suddenly wide awake as he took the document over to his desk and unrolled it, placing a heavy paper weight on one end of it and a gilded bronze and malachite inkwell on the other. There, laid out before him was an old and yellowing onion skin with miniscule writing on it, in a language he had never encountered. Something deep down inside told him it was German, but it could have been Portuguese or Greek for all he knew. There were several pages written on both sides with an old fashioned fountain pen in deep blue ink which had not faded with time. It was signed at the bottom of the last page, M. O.

"*Another mystery*" Gaspar sighed to himself, as he turned out the light and crawled into his bunk.

CHAPTER 18

PARTY TIME

PULLING HIMSELF TOGETHER SUNDAY MORNING, GASPAR RAN DOWNSTAIRS IN TIME FOR BREAKFAST, before heading to church with his mom, Alex and Alex's parents, Angela and Felix. Gaspar found himself the center of attention as he arrived at the church. Word about the capture of the jewel thieves and the return of the purloined sparklers had hit the papers, in which Gaspar had been credited by the police as the person responsible for the success of the operation. Walking up to the church with Alex by his side, grown men stopped him to shake his hand and pat him on the back, while kids his own age gave him the thumbs up. To Gaspar's discomfort old women smiled and nodded at him from a distance and young girls ran up to him to giggle at him idiotically. When he and Alex entered the church, those assembled turned around as one to get a glimpse of the young hero and his sidekick, as they took their seats near the altar. Although he continued walking down the aisle, he really wanted to turn around and run. The minute the service was over, Gaspar and Alex made a beeline for the exit only to be stopped by Father Mulchahey, who congratulated him on a job well done, while blessing him and Alex with holy water. Finally reaching the old woody station wagon, after a lot of hoo-ha from total strangers who waited for him along the way, he and Alex jumped in and with Lamar at the wheel headed for Llojeta and Villa Gaspar.

When he got there the kids crowded around him, asking a million questions, wanting to hear the story of the capture and arrest first-hand from the hero himself. Gaspar promised to fill them in with all the gory details at dinner. Gaspar had put a lot of time and trouble into the club's activities and he didn't want his recent triumph to interfere with his well laid plans. Besides the usual fun and games, Gaspar had little-by-little stepped up his friends' social education too. He'd very cleverly hired Mr. Mariscal Martini from the Naples Yacht Club to teach his pals how to dance. Martini was also adept at the finer social graces, such as table manners and how to elegantly eat asparagus and artichokes, like a man of the world. Martini happily showed the gang manly ways to address a lady, and he even brought in his personal tailor to show the boys proper ways to dress for all types of occasions. Gaspar also asked Mariscal to comment on each boy's appearance and how they carried themselves. He taught them all the best dance moves for rumba, cha-cha, foxtrot, waltz, Charleston, swing, big apple, and even the old-fashioned twist. Herbert Jefferson, who was the best modern dancer amongst them, offered to teach them all the newest moves which he'd picked up off the latest music videos out of Los Angeles, New York and London. Best of all, Mr. Martini sat in on their dinners, their roundtable discussions and their old movie screenings. He commented along the way on what they were watching and what the actors were doing right or wrong, right down to the ladies' diamond clips, and the men's badly-folded pocket handkerchiefs.

Gaspar had also hired Miss Adele Ryan, every Wednesday, to work with the girls. Her lessons didn't sound easy as far as Gaspar was concerned. The poor old wench had the thankless task of teaching June's *silly, dismal-dreaming, dizzy-eyed* friends how to walk and talk, how to sit demurely with their ankles crossed, and how to flirt in a ladylike way. Miss Ryan also brought in experts to introduce the girls to cosmetics and how to use them and also an elocution coach. She hired beauticians to help them model their hair in styles more becoming to their individual types. She even brought in sales associates from Candy's Department Store to teach the girls what styles of clothing were acceptable for different occasions and social situations. Miss Ryan went as far as to bring in a French chef who they could watch and work with in the kitchen to learn a few basics about preparing simple food. June told Gaspar what Miss Ryan told the girls … "These are a few fine points that you ladies might not receive from Miss Pruit,"referring to the frumpy home economics teacher at Jackson.

Once a month, Mr. Martini and Miss Ryan got together for a cotillion in the ballroom at Villa Gaspar with both boys and girls in attendance. On alternating months the cotillion would be held either on Sunday nights with the boys hosting the girls or Wednesday nights with the girls hosting the boys. For these evenings parents were invited to sit on the sidelines and sip punch while watching their well-dressed youngsters … boys in blazers and ties, girls in pretty party dresses and white gloves, dancing.

CHAPTER 19

THE PLEASURE OF YOUR COMPANY

Weeks had passed since the jewel thieves had been thwarted and the sparklers returned to their rightful owners. But those events struck only a minor note in the symphony of Gaspar's life or the life of tiny Perdido Isle itself. Weekdays for Gaspar and his friends were filled with school and sports. Saturdays were spent goofing off, and Sundays were packed with interesting past times at the clubhouse in Llojeta. After the passing of several more Sundays, Gaspar decided that the time was right for the boys to give a dance of their own. Friday, November 27th was decided on. It was not a coincidence that the 27th was also Uncle Charlie's birthdate. Everyone in the class was invited including their parents. The party was to be black tie, and would

185

commence at 10:00 in the evening. Midnight supper would be served. Gaspar arranged to bring in the dance band from The Grande Hotel Floride for the occasion. Invitations were sent out, valet parkers hired and a caterer was selected to provide the food and service for the evening. June volunteered her gals to do the flowers but Gaspar told her that he preferred to use the florist in town, because he could tell them what to do and he had some specific ideas he'd like to see carried out. Gaspar also made it clear that this was the boys' night, and that they were the hosts. He told June that if they wanted to, the girls could host the next one.

Forty kids were invited and eighty parents. Most of the guests ate dinner at home, but some gave small dinner parties before the dance and invited their friends. Gaspar, Elvira and Peter invited the core group of Alex, Kevin, Pat, Sancho and Mark for dinner at La Rinconada along with their dates, their parents and Mr. Martini and Miss Ryan. Dinner for twenty-eight was set up in La Rinconada's dining room. At 9:30 Gaspar and Alex and their dates, June and Alicia left to be on hand at Villa Gaspar when the guests started arriving. Lamar drove the quartet to the dance in his limo, then went back to pick up Elvira and Peter.

The party was a huge success. All of the kids, dressed to the nines, behaved brilliantly, much to the credit of Miss Ryan and Mr. Martini, who stood proudly on the side lines and took credit for what the kids' parents were witnessing. The parents stood in knots, meeting and greeting each other, pointing out their youngsters, and marveling at how well behaved, well read, well spoken, and opinionated on current affairs they had all become. Also present were the class's teachers from Jackson, who wanted to take credit for what they saw, but knew that none of what was going on tonight had been their doing. On the stroke of midnight, with the orchestra in full swing, Mrs. Hobart opened the doors to the terrace which had been enclosed with clear plastic. This is where Gaspar had planned to serve midnight supper, and the buffet tables placed there groaned under the repast that he and Mrs. Hobart had directed the caterer to prepare and serve. Boys helped girls and their parents heap dishes with the delicious tidbits that Gaspar had ordered. Little tables set up around the crowded dance floor were used for dining, while others balanced their dishes on their laps in the sitting room, media room, library, pub and game rooms. The dining room had also been opened, and there, displayed on the large mahogany table, was a dessert buffet to rival any party mis-en-scene Hollywood could have imagined even in its most tinseled days. Lamar had positioned himself behind the soda fountain in the pub and kept busy all night fixing gooey ice cream desserts and drinks for Gaspar's young friends and quite a few of the adults too. It was three in the morning when the last guest left, and Gaspar and Alex could proclaim success to Elvira, Peter, and dear Mrs. Hobart.

CHAPTER 20

THE POSTMORTEM

AROUND TEN THE NEXT MORNING, ALEX LET HIMSELF INTO LA RINCONADA WITH SLEEP STILL IN HIS EYES and joined Gaspar and Elvira in the upstairs sitting room where Elvira was watching Alfred Hitchcock's *Notorious* starring Cary Grant, Ingrid Bergman and Claude Rains. The film was on TCM in glorious black and white, as Gaspar wearing a robe greeted his friend groggily at the top of the stairs. The two boys sat down with Elvira and watched the Nazi spy thriller together while drinking hot chocolate and gorging themselves on cinnamon toast, which Elvira had brought up on a tray from the kitchen. After the movie ended they all rehashed last night's party with a lot of hilarity and happiness. Alex and Elvira congratulated Gaspar heartily on a job well done.

"What's next, Gasp?" Alex asked. "Something tells me you have bigger plans for the club than a dance and midnight supper."

"Funny you should ask, Al. I do have an idea, and let me tell you … it's a pretty big one."

"Wha-da-ya have in mind?" Alex and Elvira were all ears.

"I want to bring in a speaker, a well-known speaker, to talk to the people of Perdido Isle about a subject of importance. We've already discussed current affairs and topics of world-wide importance taken from the headlines. All of that was well and good but now I want to do something sensational, something metaphysical, something unexpected. I want to bring in an expert on extra sensory perception and parallel universes, or something like that. Someone controversial and unpredictable … to say the least." Gaspar waited for their reactions.

"Where are you going to find someone like that?" Elvira asked. "There are so many charlatans out there, Gaspar. You need to be careful, less you end up with egg on your face," his mother warned.

"Yeah, Gasp. Remember what happened to Houdini," Alex agreed.

"I'm not talking about magic tricks or smoke and mirrors, Al. Anyway, let's not all get excited. It's just an idea, something I've got on my mind. If it happens, it happens. Only time will tell." Gaspar turned his attention back to the credits for the next movie, which had just started to roll. Watching the movie, his mind wandered to the parchment he'd found in the jeweled dagger and its significance.

Alex ignored Gaspar's most recent revelation or could he call it insanity and changed the subject. "Wha-da-ya-goin-ta-do the rest of the day?" he asked his pal.

"I don't know," Gaspar said, now preoccupied with the next film, which involved more dirty Nazis running amuck. The film, which was one of his favorite comedies starring Jack Benny and Carole Lombard was *"To Be or Not To Be"*, which Gaspar looked forward to as a laugh riot.

VRIL POWER

GASPAR HAD SPENT A RESTLESS FRIDAY NIGHT, TOSS-ING AND TURNING ON HIS BUNK IN HIS FANTASY bedroom, which had been outfitted in the 1920s by Uncle Charlie to look like the captain's cabin on a pirate's ship. When Gaspar finally woke up on Saturday morning, he was not at all refreshed. His dreams had been peopled with Germans in uniform, police dogs, U-boats and elaborate beaux arts buildings crowded together like in the European cities he'd seen in books, magazines and the movies. The whole night had been fraught with mysterious activities, which had endlessly played over and over in his sleep. His only point of reference for this vivid and frustrating dream was a mash-up between two of his favorite old black and white films ... *Casablanca* and *Notorious*. It seemed that Ingrid Bergman had played a major role in the back and forth of all the Nazi comings and goings that still groggily filled his head. He hoped an invigorating shower would wake him up and help clear his mind.

He'd been researching for weeks, trying to come up with an exciting and different idea to present to the people of Perdido Isle as part of the seminar series which he sponsored through his clubhouse at Villa Gaspar. Try as he may he still hadn't come up with anything tangible or controversial that he felt would really shake people up.

As he stepped out of the shower, he was happy to see his best friend and side kick Alex Mendoza stepping into the room. It was always open house at La Rinconada and Alex was welcome anytime, day or night.

"Gasp, are you just getting up? What's going on, man, it's not like you to sleep in on a Saturday morning. I thought maybe you'd like to go fishing with me?"

"Morning, Al," Gaspar greeted his pal as he toweled off. "No fishing for me today, bro."

"What's up, didn't you sleep well last night?"

"I was up all night, man. So many weird dreams. I just want to hang out here and be lazy."

"How 'bout us taking our bikes out to goof off. All the guys will be down at the ol' swimmin' hole, and we can end up there," Alex suggested.

"Tell you what, Al. I've got something on my mind. I still haven't come up with an idea for that lecture series I told you about so many weeks ago. I want to give it one more try on the internet … and if I'm lucky, I'll meet you guys out at the pond for a swim later. Right now, I need to do some research."

"Research, on Saturday?" Alex was horrified. "Sounds like school!" he blurted. I'll be swimmin' with the gang when you come to your senses," he said, leaving Gaspar to get dressed and do his thing.

Gaspar was a man of action. He got some breakfast from the kitchen and took it upstairs to his office and got right to work. He began again to set up a symposium to be given to the people of Perdido Isle. He still had Señora Martinez de Gozz's jeweled dagger on his mind, and he still felt that it had been stolen from the castle of Montegufoni in Italy. All of his time had been taken up with his symposium idea, and he hadn't had a chance to follow up on what was probably more important. His mind then traveled to Buenos Aires where the Señora was from. He just kept clicking from one subject to the other … which led to Aryan domination, Nazi vampires, occult practices and secret societies. And then, *at last*, there it was … a subject he would like to learn more about, *Vril Power*, whatever that was. After reading as much as he could about *Vril*, he could tell that it would be a controversial subject suitable for discussion on Perdido Isle. He figured that he could easily show both sides of whatever the argument might be, while at the same time exposing the world powers complete idiocy. Having made up his mind, he hoped he could find someone who was not only an expert on the subject of Vril Power, but even better, *a believer*. Gaspar decided to find the preeminent authority and invite him or her to speak on Perdido Isle. *That ought to make people's hair stand on end*, he thought, as visions of Indiana Jones and the Lost Ark filled his head.

Researching thoroughly, he came up with a real winner. The Argentinian medium Maria Orsic, a famous seer and an outspoken promoter of Vril Power. Gaspar, instantly composed an email to the woman, inviting her to speak in early December at a private club on Perdido Isle, Florida, all expenses paid, first class. It wasn't fifteen minutes before Gaspar received a reply.

> *Dear Mr. Brown,*
> *Yes, I would be honored to speak to your group. Please send me the dates, air flight information, and other pertinent details. I speak perfect English so no translator will be necessary. I travel with four other women known as the Vrilerinne.*
>
> *Sincerely,*
> *Maria Orsic.*

Gaspar couldn't believe his good fortune so he decided to hightail it down to the swimmin' hole to tell Alex.

Jumping off his snazzy red flyer, he ran through the jungle towards the lagoon which was fed by the high tide off the Gulf of Mexico. When he reached the area, all the guys started calling to him. "It's about time you got here, come on in, the water's fine," they hollered, along with all the usual cajoling and cat calls that accompanied every boy's arrival on Saturday afternoons. Joining in the fun, Gaspar quickly pulled off his clothes and jumped into the fray. Before long a major round of Marco Polo had ensued, with a lot of splashing, diving and running around the perimeter of the lagoon by boys trying not to be *it*.

Dragging himself onto the beach, Gaspar flopped down next to Alex, who had also quit the game, out of breath from dodging the guy who was *it*.

"Did you finish your research, Gasp?" Alex asked disinterestedly.

"Yeah, Al. I did, and I've finally come up with *something hot*," Gaspar told his pal.

"Wha-da-ya-mean, *hot*?" Alex wanted to know.

"A controversial speaker on a controversial subject, exactly what I've been looking for … it's called Vril Power." Gaspar announced enthusiastically.

"Never heard of it," was Alex's unimpressed reaction. "What the *drivelswiggers* is Vril Power and how'd you find out about it?"

"Well, I went online, and I was looking for something interesting. I still have that jeweled dagger on my mind and the lady from Argentina who it was robbed from. I just know it was stolen by some dirty Nazi from the castle of Montegufoni, but I haven't been able to verify that connection yet. So I started looking up Nazi loot, and Nazis in Argentina. That led to the Ahnenerbe Society, the Thule Society, the Vril Society, and then Vril Power and Nazi vampires, and secret hideouts in the Antarctic, and the South Pole. Well you know how it is when you start a search on the web and how, before you know it, you've ended up with some weird porn site which you never wanted to go to in the first place."

"What was it like?" Alex asked anxiously, all of sudden more interested than ever.

"What was what like?" Gaspar asked innocently.

"The porn site!" Alex started to get excited.

"Forget about the porn site, Al. I couldn't be bothered with it … women in black leather, and German shepherd dogs, and shiny black boots. Forget about it, it wasn't important, let alone interesting."

Alex suddenly looked crestfallen and feigned boredom.

"What I ended up with Al, was Vril Power. I don't know exactly what it is, but I found the worldwide expert on the subject and she has agreed to come to Perdido Isle and talk to us about it, just before Christmas this year."

"Is she good lookin'?" Alex asked, his interest revived.

"Al, she's a babe. Wait till you see her and she's bringing four more babes with her."

"How old is she, Gasp? Our age?" Alex hoped.

"I don't know, but from her picture I guess she's probably twenty," Gaspar figured.

"Oh, Gasp. She's ancient. Couldn't you get someone younger?"

"Al, who do you know our age that's an expert on anything except maybe goofing off. Come on, get with it. I want to bring someone really bright who's a world-renowned authority, in some subject that nobody has ever heard of … and this is it. Vril Power." Gaspar boasted.

"Whatever you say, Gasp. I just hope this doesn't come back and bite you in the ass."

• • •

That night Uncle Charlie, or more precisely his ghost, stopped by the captain's cabin for a long overdue visit and Gaspar told him what he was up to.

"You're always playing with fire, Gasp!"

Gaspar was thrilled that Uncle Charlie obviously approved.

"Just make sure and wear your asbestos underwear that night," the old ghost warned. "This is the kind of fun that could end up *biting you in the ass*," he echoed Al's warning, "or even worse, burn you bad." Uncle Charlie laughed his head off. "Fire in the hold!" he cried, before disappearing through the door.

CHAPTER 22

THE MYSTERY OF THE JEWELED DAGGER

AFTER SOLVING THE MYSTERY OF THE SEMINOLE SPRINGS, THERE WERE STILL SO MANY QUESTIONS YET to be answered. For example, the jeweled dagger that he had retrieved for Señora Martinez de Gozz and the mysterious document he'd found hidden in the secret compartment deep inside the dagger's handle. It was written by hand in a foreign language and he had yet to have it translated. Gaspar didn't like being in the dark about these kinds of things. He decided to make an appointment to visit his friend Captain Morgan down at the Calaluna Police Station after school on Monday and see what he could find out.

The minute the bell rang, Gaspar ran out of class and went straight to the police station. He'd told his best friend Alex that he'd meet him later, back at La Rinconada and to send Lamar straight back to pick him up at headquarters. Striding into the precinct, Gaspar's friend Sergeant O'Malley greeted the teenager and told him that the captain was waiting for him in his office.

"Good afternoon, Gaspar," Captain Morgan greeted his teenaged friend. "Come and sit down. It's good to see you looking so spry after our ordeal at the Seminole Springs. That was quite a coup you pulled off, my friend," the captain beamed his congratulations.

"Glad I could help out, captain," Gaspar replied.

"What can I do for you today?" Captain Morgan asked.

"I'm wondering if Señora Martinez de Gozz has come down to claim her stolen gems, and if the ringleader, whatever his name is, has come in contact with any of the loot since being arrested?" Gaspar asked.

"No, Herman the ring leader of the gang is locked up tight as a drum, and the Argentinian lady hasn't been down yet. Why do you ask?" the captain wondered.

"I would like to observe first the ring leader, and then Señora de Gozz to see what they do when they are left alone with the jeweled dagger." Gaspar said matter-of-factly.

"That's a very odd request, Gaspar. Why would you want to observe them doing that?" The captain asked, baffled.

"Indulge me, please, sir. Put them in the interrogation room with the two-way mirror so that we can observe them. I think we will discover another piece of the puzzle," Gaspar assured the policeman.

"Whatever you say, Gaspar. I can't imagine that it will do any harm to carry out your interesting experiment. But when we're done, I'd like a full explanation," the captain insisted. With that, Captain Morgan gave instructions to Sergeant O'Malley to bring in the evidence and bring in the prisoner. While waiting for O'Malley to do that, he telephoned The Grand Hotel Floride and spoke with Señora Martinez de Gozz, requesting her immediate presence at police headquarters to help identify her stolen jewelry.

The prisoner, who Captain Morgan referred to as the ring leader, was brought into the interrogation room by Sergeant O'Malley, who took a seat across the table from the crook. O'Malley proceeded to remove the jeweled dagger from inside a box marked exhibit "A" and then asked the prisoner some very unimportant questions.

"When did you first learn that Señora Martinez de Gozz was in possession of this magnificent object?" O'Malley asked the prisoner, who only grunted a guttural response by way of refusing to answer any questions.

"What did you intend to do with this object after you got it away from Perdido Isle? Sell it, melt it down, keep it for yourself?" The sergeant tried in vain to get an intelligible response from the criminal, but to no avail.

"At what point did you plan to take the stolen merchandise off of Perdido Isle, and where were you planning to take it and why?" Gaspar, listening in on the other side of the two-way mirror, had to bite his lip to stop from laughing out loud at the stupidity of the questions and O'Malley's feigned discomfort when the prisoner refused to answer, other than to growl and let out a burp or two.

With that the telephone rang on cue, and Sergeant O'Malley answered it. Captain Morgan was on the other end and asked O'Malley to leave the room as if he had been called away on an errand, and to leave the jeweled dagger in plain sight on top of the table.

"Listen, bub," O'Malley addressed the prisoner, "that was the captain and he needs me in a hurry. That's the way it is around here ... hurry, hurry, hurry. It's driving me crazy. Just sit tight, I'll be right back," he said, getting up from the table and stepping out of the room, locking the door behind him.

Not wasting a second after the door was shut, the prisoner jumped up and grabbed the jeweled dagger. Feeling around the end of the handle, he found the sapphire thumb piece that released the mechanism, which opened the ruby-encrusted butt of the dagger's handle. Frantically he slipped his finger into the void, then he shook the dagger ferociously before next holding it up to his right eye to better see if anything was inside. Not believing that it was empty, he began thumping the butt end of the weapon against his open left palm, hoping to dislodge the document stored inside, but nothing happened.

"What's he doing?" Captain Morgan asked Gaspar, from their position behind the two-way mirror in the observation room.

"He's looking for something that's supposed to be hidden there, captain. Maybe it's a note or microfilm, or some loose stones that he had hidden there or that were supposed to be hidden there?"

"How'd you know that, Gasp?" the Captain queried.

"It just seemed logical that there might be something inside the dagger that made it more than just a valuable *objet de virtue*. Perhaps the handle contained a treasure map, or a handful of diamonds, or illegal drugs ... who knows." Gaspar smiled. "Whatever was supposed to be in there, that guy looks mighty upset that he hasn't found it. Now I can't wait to see what Señora Martinez de Gozz does when she sees it for the first time since it was stolen." Gaspar wondered.

"We're expecting the lady soon," the captain told him. "She should be here directly."

Shortly, an elegant bird-like old lady was escorted into the room by Sergeant O'Malley. The stage had already been set for a dramatic reunion for the South American lady and her precious bijoux. Having escorted her into the room, the telephone rang almost immediately and Sergeant O'Malley excused himself for a minute to do Captain Morgan's bidding. As soon as he'd closed the door behind him, Gaspar and the captain observed Señora de Gozz jump like a tigress across the table, ignoring all the sparkling rings, bracelets, earrings and necklaces to grab the jeweled dagger. Instantly she fingered the latch which sprang the ruby lid on the butt of the handle, and felt around frantically with her long fine-boned aristocratic fingers. Feeling nothing, she turned the object over and banged it against the palm of her hand just like the ring leader had done a few minutes previously, but nothing came out. Furious, she snapped the lid closed and placed the dagger back where Sergeant O'Malley had left it. Then, not satisfied, she replayed the entire scene one more time for good measure, just to assure herself that the handle was indeed empty. Gaspar nearly split a gut holding back his laughter at the sight of the silly distracted and obviously confused, but now furious lady's reaction to discovering her loss. With that, Sergeant O'Malley stepped back into the room and asked if the lady had had sufficient time to look over the stolen jewelry and if they indeed matched her stolen pieces. She said that she had, and that they did, and then asked if she could take them home with her.

"Not just yet, dear lady," the sergeant replied. "We need to hold these as evidence against the captured crooks. If you don't mind, we will just keep these here for another week or two."

"*Ay, que barbaridad,*" was her response in Spanish, as she flounced out of the room.

"Well, Gaspar, that was very interesting. How did you know about that secret compartment and what do you think you've learned from this experiment?" Captain Morgan asked him suspiciously.

"Let me answer that question another day, captain. If you don't mind, I need to get back to La Rinconada now. I have a lot of research to do, so that I can give you a coherent answer. Thank you for indulging me today. My eyes have now been opened as well," Gaspar told the policeman as he left the room.

CHAPTER 23

THE TRANSLATION

O N THE FOLLOWING SATURDAY MORNING, GASPAR
CALLED ALEX AND ASKED HIM TO COME OUTSIDE.
"I need some help," he told his pal. "There's a new
development in the mystery of the jeweled dagger that
I want to tell you about."

When Alex arrived a few minutes later, he discovered
Lamar waiting out in front with the motor of his big
silver limo running. "What's up, Gasp?"

"Jump in," Gaspar called from the open window.
"We've got an errand to run."

"Aren't we goin' to meet the guys at the ol' swimmin'
hole today?" Alex asked.

"Not this morning, Al. I need you to help me solve a
mystery." Gaspar told him cryptically.

Alex was surprised to see that Gaspar had closed the window between themselves and Lamar. He'd experienced the window closed a couple of times before and understood it as a sign that important things were about to be revealed to him by his best friend. As the car raced across the bridge that connected Perdido Isle to the mainland, Gaspar filled Alex in on the business at hand.

"Al, we're going to see a man in Coral County called Dr. Gottlieb. He teaches German and other European languages at the university there. I need him to translate some documents I've found and I want you to take notes. I don't want him to know too much about us, so we're not going to use our real names. I'll be Kevin Geer, and you'll be Joseph Cotton." Gaspar chose the names of his two favorite actors. "You take notes like crazy, okay, and I'll do the talking."

Always loyal and willing to go along with whatever Gaspar suggested, Alex just sat back and nodded his acquiescence. "How long is this going to take," he drawled, feigning boredom by closing his eyes for a catnap.

Gaspar had seen this act before and didn't bother with an answer. Besides, he had too much on his mind to take notice of anything except the quest he was currently on.

After a short drive, the car pulled into the development where Dr. Gottlieb lived. Gaspar put down the dividing window between the passenger compartment and the driver and said, "Lamar, when you get to the house, point it out to us but drive past it and park around the block. Al and I will walk back to the house, and then walk back and meet you around the corner when we're done with our interview."

"*That be the howse rawte therr, boss,*" Lamar pointed out a simple yellow-plastered bungalow, and continued driving down the street and parking around the corner.

"Wait here, Lamar. We'll be right back," Gaspar called before slamming the door shut.

Walking back to the Gottlieb house, Gaspar and Alex strode up the concrete walkway to the front door and rang the bell. What they heard was a chime that sounded just like Big Ben in London. Gaspar took it as a sign, an omen, since it was exactly like he'd seen and heard in his favorite Basil Rathbone, Sherlock Holmes mysteries.

When Dr. Gottlieb opened the door, Gaspar introduced himself as Kevin Geer, and Alex as Joseph Cotton … both names that he knew would sound familiar and hopefully convincing to the old professor.

"Dr. Gottlieb, I've brought you some old notes written in a foreign language by my great uncle, which I would like translated. I think they are written in German, but only you would know that, sir. Here they are, Dr. Gottlieb," he said, handing over the documents. "Now if you would just translate what you see here, verbatim. Joe and I will take notes."

Dr. Gottlieb looked over the Xerox copies of the handwritten documents that Gaspar had found in the handle of the jeweled dagger. After a while the professor exclaimed, "*Oh my!*"

"Please, just read it out loud, sir, in English," Gaspar urged the German scholar to action.

> *"In 1944 there were two landings on the beach of San Clemente del Tuyu near Mar del Plata (Argentina) of two German submarines carrying Martin Bormann and his 'treasure'. The dates were February 7th 1944 and July 18th 1944. Bormann and his crew unloaded many heavy trunks with 'Secret Police' written on the side of each. The trunks were taken to the nearby ranch of Lahusen. The man who coordinated all this was Ernst Kaltenbrunner, the Third Reich's chief of the secret police. The trunks contained 187,692,400 German marks, 17,576,500 U.S. dollars, 4,682,500 pounds sterling, 24,976,500 Swiss francs, 8,379,000 Dutch florins, 54,963,000 French francs, 17,280,000 Belgian francs, 2,511 kilograms of gold and 4,638 carats of diamonds and precious stones. This does not include what came into Argentina on the* Graf Spee, *in 1939, which was the 'mother lode'."*

"Wow," Gaspar whistled.

"Whew-wee," Alex seconded.

"Shall I continue, gentlemen?" Dr. Gottlieb pleaded.

"Carry on," Gaspar insisted.

Bormann was too stingy with his 'treasure', which annoyed his cohorts and little by little three of his henchmen 'committed suicide' … in addition to the mysterious death of Evita's brother, Juancito Duarte, who was representing the Perons with this transaction in Argentina."

"Peron gave the German military attaché in Argentina 8000 Argentine passports without signatures or fingerprints, and 100,000 Argentine identification cards that were signed and sealed by the police of Argentina —also without photos or fingerprints. Seventy-seven of the German elite—the Kroops, the Thyssens, the Simenses—had prepared their financial and physical future in Argentina on August 10th, 1944. They sent all the gold and currency they had at that time and moved shortly thereafter near Buenos Aires."

"I was witness to what was brought from Germany in the Graf Spee, *which was even bigger. Many millions of pounds of Nazi gold was sent across the Atlantic to the coast of Patagonia by submarine. The funds were sent to finance major Nazi figures planning to move to Argentina. But what I write about is only a small amount of the actual dispatch of vast wealth sent from Germany to the Argentine via Juan Peron. My evidence*

can be corroborated by sailors who sailed and transferred the loot from the Graf Spee *to the mainland. Other evidence is supported by Wilfred von Oven, who worked with Joseph Goebbels, Hitler's propaganda chief, and is now a writer for the German-language newspapers in Argentina. My revelations will be uncomfortable for many in Germany, Switzerland and Argentina, as well as for those in high office inside the Vatican. I accuse and have direct evidence against His Holiness Pope Pius XII, who aided the process by telling various senior clergy to collaborate with the organizers, notably Bishop Alois Hudal, an anti-Semitic pro-Nazi who runs Santa Maria dell 'Anima, the church of the German community in Rome, as well as Monsignor Krunoslav Draganovic. The Vatican has long been linked to the organization, which funneled Nazis and their wealth to South America and through Peron to Argentina. Peron was Argentina's military attaché in Rome before the Second World War, and was an intense admirer of Benito Mussolini and the man who encouraged Nazi immigration to Argentina. Peron employed Rodolfo Freede, the son of a businessman and paymaster for the German spy network in Argentina. Freede had charge of the funds sent by submarine. He was helped by Werner Koenecke, who spied indiscriminately for the British, Germans and Argentinians, and who was married to Freede's sister Lillia. Koenecke was arrested by the Argentine political police but released after a few months on Peron's orders."*

"Alberto Cagliani, Archbishop of the Argentine city of Rosarita and later of Buenos Aires, is often named as a link in the chain which guided the Nazis to their new life. He helped to cement deals between Peron and those fleeing their war crimes in Europe. Cagliani visited Pius XII in Rome to collect his cardinal's red hat and was closely associated with the Argentine military dictator. The remains of a German U-boat landing can be found in Patagonia, deep in southern Argentina. Huge amounts of monies were transferred to Argentina in order to be used for espionage and propaganda. The friendship of Colonel Peron with a powerful banker who played a crucial role in the transfer of funds to Argentina, was accelerated by the detention of a man sent by Peron to make a pact with the Reich. Once released from German custody, this banker's son was appointed private secretary of Peron. A real Odessa was set up around Peron. Criminals like Eichmann, Mengele, Priebke were summoned regularly to Argentina. A German captain became the director of a mysterious office in Berne and another one a few steps from the Vatican. Helped by the Vatican and the silence of the United States, Peron arranged the transfer of great fortunes and also the escape of the most evil Nazis to Argentina, creating a tangled web of crimes, criminals, treasure and greed heretofore never

seen outside of Bolshevik Russia. Newt Frankhauser, an ex-Hitler financier created a systematic plan to destroy all evidence of these crimes and, with Peron, he managed to definitely establish himself at the top of Argentine and international economic power. This story has been kept secret, but someday the man must pay. Frankhauser was the leader of Himmler's Ahnenerbe, and he's the man responsible for the theft of the famous Necronomicon *from the Bibliothèque Nationale in Paris, during the Nazi occupation of that city. It is possible that the rare book might have survived the RAF bombing campaign of the Ahnenerbe Headquarters in Berlin in 1943 and that the secret group took it with them when they subsequently relocated to an underground location in Antarctica. I understand that the hidden Nazi gold was sent to a safe place in Argentina as part of their funding, though I have never been able to verify the rumor. All I can verify is that the gold, the book, and other rare treasure, and occult materials, were delivered inland from the coast, and have never been seen since.*

Signed M.O. 1944

"I'm afraid that is all, sir. I don't know what to make of it. Do you?" Dr. Gottlieb asked Gaspar.

"That was great, Dr. Gottlieb. Thank you very much. How much do I owe you for the translation?" Gaspar asked.

"Oh, twenty dollars will be fine," Dr. Gottlieb replied.

"Here you are, sir. I appreciate your work." Gaspar handed the man a crisp twenty from his pocket.

Gaspar folded up the photocopied documents and placed them back in his jeans' pocket, before taking his leave of the professor. With infinite ease, Kevin Geer and Joseph Cotton, aka Gaspar Brown and Alex Mendoza walked to Gottlieb's front door and let themselves out. Hitting the sidewalk, they sauntered down the block in the opposite direction from which they had come, and went around the block the long way to where Lamar was waiting for them. Back inside the limo, with the glass divider again closed between Lamar and themselves, Alex blurted out "I don't understand what all this is about, Gasp. What's next? Enlighten me!"

"You *ragtag miscreant*. I've just alerted you to the presence of *hidden Nazi gold*! I'm expecting you to help me find it, before some other *blistering baboon* gets to it!"

"Where will we begin looking? What shall we pack? Which of our other *ragtag miscreant* friends will you take along on this mission? Where do you think this hidden Nazi gold resides?" Alex asked in rapid succession.

"We'll probably find it in some secret Nazi forest, outside of Buenos Aires, Al … How am I supposed to know?" Gaspar answered testily.

"Or maybe we should look in the Vatican," Alex suggested.

"Yeah, like the Pope's really gonna let us in and allow us to snoop around amongst his Leonardos. Get real, Al. Besides they'll never let us in there since neither of us has been to confession in years. That fact alone sets us up for failure at the Vatican, so forget about it!" Gaspar chuckled. "Heck, we've never even been altar boys!"

"I heard somewhere on the internet that the Nazis often covered their gold ingots in Swiss chocolate for safekeeping. Maybe we should start looking in all the Swiss chocolate shops in Argentina." Alex suggested incredulously.

"Are you sure you're not mixing up chocolate Godiva truffles wrapped in gold foil with hidden Nazi gold?" Gaspar scoffed at his friend's delusions.

"Maybe the Nazis made a secret map and hid it within the frames of a movie, like your favorites *Notorious* or *Casablanca*, or even in a Bugs Bunny cartoon. They were pretty clever, those Nazi guys!" Alex insisted.

"If we could only find a real Nazi. He could probably lead us right to the mother lode. We'd have to be careful, of course. We don't want to end up leading him to the treasure instead of the other way around and then find him pointing a luger at our heads, while he takes off with all the scudi." Gaspar fantasized.

"If he's accompanied by a couple of meddling kids, like us, he'll never get away with it," Alex chuckled.

"What we really need to do is find out who M.O. is in that signed that document and how he or she got all that information," Gaspar suggested.

"Okay, so are we sailing for Argentina or for Switzerland? If the gold has been formed into ingots secreted at the center of dozens of ribbon-tied boxes of dark chocolate truffles, then it only seems right to start in Switzerland. The truffles are probably still in storage, deep within some secret Swiss chocolate cavern, stored at a controlled temperature of 98.6 degrees Fahrenheit or something like that?" Gaspar was getting into the mood of Alex's romantic fantasy.

"So you actually think that the gold's being secured by a battalion of Swiss guards, the same ones that protect the Vatican?" Alex asked. "It makes sense to me, Gasp." Alex didn't know what scenario to consider at this point, they were both having so much fun.

"Yeah, but it's been a long time since 1944, Al. By now the chocolate mines are probably haunted and filled with SS vampires and monsters like the phantoms of Hitler, Himmler, Goebbels and all the rest of their dirty criminal friends like Juan and Evita Peron. They are also probably filled with battalions of good-looking Hitler youth who help lure people like us into the caves, before the others suck our blood." Gaspar did his best to keep the ball rolling.

"What next then, Gasp?" Alex asked with a shudder.

"What's next. We haven't even decided what's first!" Gaspar interjected.

"You tell me, brother," Alex insisted.

"Let's start from the beginning again, Al. This time, *no nonsense*," Gaspar warned. "I want you to pretend that you're in a room, but there's no Nazi gold in it."

"Are there exits to the west and south?" Alex asked in all seriousness.

"West and south! I have no idea, Al. What difference does it make? Now pay attention, *you mummy wrapped in bacon."* Gaspar started to raise his voice.

"Let's approach this from a different angle, Al," Gaspar calmed down. "Now, supposing everyone knows that the hidden Nazi gold was recovered from the remnants of a German base in the Queen Maud Land area of Antarctica around 1947. Queen Maud Land was where H. R. Puff-n-stuff discovered the Isle of Ick, and *The Lost City of Diminishing Returns* from the book of the same name. As you already know, Al, *The Lost City of Diminishing Returns* was an early version of a scam *Necronomicon* that contained secret information, which had fallen into the hands of the Burnell Society. You know ... those scary guys from Pasadena, California who practiced money worship and who, unable to take a joke, took the book literally and immediately funded an initial survey of the Queen Maud Land area sometime around 1949. As WWII came to an end, the remaining Nazi gold along with certain occult artifacts were successfully hidden in a secret lair belonging to Martin Bormann in Queen Maud Land in April 1944. The weakened Nazis sent the *Graf Spee*, their finest battleship, to Queen Maud Land to pick up all the remaining gold and treasure and bring it to Argentina. Their mission having been completed, it is said that the *Graf Spee* was scuttled in the middle of the Rio de la Plata, as a reminder to all the Porteños living there, that Buenos Aires was from this day forward to be considered as just another suburb of Berlin. History has officially attributed the sinking to a naval battle between the German battleship *Graf Spee* and the Uruguayan Navy. But that story has never held much water. My dad told me all about it." Gaspar added with authority.

"Well, Gasp, I've been listening to all your theories with awe. I actually watched a show on the History Channel about this very subject."

"The History Channel … my dad always used to call it The Hitler Channel, 'cause most of the stuff they broadcast is about Hitler and the Nazis." Gaspar chuckled.

"Yeah, well, in the show I saw, they pointed out an interesting adjunct to the story involving the scuttling of the *Graf Spee*. On TV they said that it actually went down on the Uruguay side of the Rio de la Plata, which gives credence to the story about the Uruguayan Navy's involvement. They said that the surviving crew never repatriated back to Germany after the war, choosing instead to settle in an Argentine town named Villa General Belgrano. They showed the town, which looked like a Bavarian Alpine village, and apparently the town people celebrate Oktoberfest every year at something called the National Beer Festivity. Gasp, we have to go to that festival when we get down there!" Alex enthused.

"Wow, Al. That was a good one, I can't believe you know so much about this already. We need to look up that episode on YouTube or Netflix or something!" Gaspar made a mental note.

"Supposedly," Alex continued, "the remaining survivors of the *Graf Spee* used to get together every year on the anniversary of the sinking, to toast the *Graf Spee's* captain, who famously did not give the Nazi salute, but a naval salute instead, at the funeral for the crewmen killed in the alleged battle."

"Wow, Al, you really were paying attention, weren't you?" Gaspar was impressed.

"Gasp, I also read somewhere that in 1947 Admiral Byrd commanded an expedition to find and explore those secret Antarctic Nazi bases. The story is that he removed not only the gold but some previously unknown secret weapons, which may or may not have been ray guns disguised as perfume atomizers." Alex interjected, again ridiculously getting back into the fun and games.

Gaspar was starting to get a little scared of Alex's powerful imagination. He'd only asked him to write down the translation of a couple of pages of handwritten, blue-inked writing, not to give his opinion on the possibilities of finding Nazi gold in Argentina, or Bechuanaland or wherever it may be, if it existed at all. He thought he'd better nip this fantasy in the bud, but didn't want to spoil his pal's fun.

"Thank you, Al, for your incredibly clever insight," Gaspar said facetiously.

"Gasp, we're gonna have to take extra care of ourselves now that we're carrying around this big secret. We can't be too careful when dealing with dead Nazis you know. If nothing else, we want to make sure we don't fall afoul of some of their more ingenious booby traps or get caught in the sights of their historically half-blind, yet still very active German shepherd attack dogs. Those dogs are killers," Alex finished up, with a shudder.

"Good one, Al. What an imagination," Gaspar praised his pal, just as the car pulled in through the gates at La Rinconada.

"Thanks, Lamar," Gaspar called as he and Alex jumped out of the car. "We'll see you tomorrow," he said, running up the front steps and through the front door of the house with Alex hot on his heels.

CHAPTER 24

RESEARCH

W ALKING INTO THE LIBRARY THEY FOUND MARGARET
STEWART, THE LIBRARIAN AT LA RINCONADA, HARD
at work. She was delighted to see her boss and his pal
actually looking like they might want to take a book
or two off the shelves. "How may I help you fellows?"
Margaret asked, hoping to be of personal service to her
teenaged boss.

"We're working on a little bit of a mystery, Margaret,"
Gaspar said, plopping down in one of the upholstered
club chairs. "What do you know about the Nazis, that we
don't know?" Gaspar asked the maiden lady, point blank.

"Nazis at La Rinconada, heaven forbid," the old maid
responded, not understanding the question.

"Let me rephrase the question. What do you know
about the *Necronomicon*?" Gaspar asked point-blank.

"It's a fake, make believe. It's a fictional grimoire, invented and written about by the author H. P. Lovecraft and his followers." Margaret Stewart didn't miss a beat. "The *Necronomicon* was first mentioned in Lovecraft's short story, "The Hound," which he wrote in 1922 but published in 1924. Its purported author, the "Mad Arab" Abdul Alhazred, had been quoted a year earlier in Lovecraft's "The Nameless City." Among other things, the work contains an account of "The Old Ones," their history and the means for summoning them."

"Margaret, I had no idea. You're a veritable font of knowledge." Gaspar complimented her.

"How did you even hear of the *Necronomicon*?" the librarian asked him, arching her eyebrows.

"Oh, I don't really remember right now. I must have heard about it in a movie or something," Gaspar lied.

"It would have had to have been a horror film," she shuddered at the thought. "Other authors such as August Derleth and Clark Ashton Smith have cited it in their works. Lovecraft approved, believing such common allusions built up a background of evil verisimilitude. Many readers have believed it to be a real work, with booksellers and librarians receiving many requests for it. Pranksters have listed it in rare book catalogues, and a student actually smuggled a card for the *Necronomicon* into the Yale University library's card catalog."

"Wow," was all Alex had to say about that.

"Margaret, what if it isn't a work of fiction? What if the *Necronomicon* actually exists, you know, like an actual ancient document, like the tablets of the Ten Commandments or something?" Gaspar asked in all seriousness. "What if it isn't lost … what if it still exists?"

"If you could find it and prove it, I'd say you really found something of enormous value on many different levels," Margaret sniffed, dismissing the fantasy out-of-hand by going back about her business, refusing by her actions to even consider the possibility.

"Have you ever heard a rumor that the original resided in the Bibliothèque Nationale in Paris, and was stolen by the Nazis during the occupation?"

"No, I've never heard that rumor," Miss Stewart responded dryly. "Where did you hear it or are you just making it up, sir?" she asked her boss with a polite, yet impatient tone.

"I made it up, Margaret," Gaspar lied, not wanting to reveal his source.

"Very well, sir. If you need me for anything else, I'm always happy to join in the fun and games."

The only trouble with Margaret, Gaspar thought, was that she had no sense of humor. "Al, let's give Miss Stewart some space and go to my office upstairs where we can both jump on a computer at the same time," Gaspar suggested.

Once upstairs in the privacy of his office, Gaspar and Alex continued their crazy plans to uncover the mystery of the old document.

"Let's digest the translated document you wrote out," Gaspar said. "Write this down, Al. We'll make a list of pertinent facts and divide them up between us to get even more information to work from."

"First, we need to find out who M.O. is that wrote the document." Gaspar pondered his course of action.

"Second, we need to find San Clemente del Tuyu on a map, near the Mar del Plata which I have a feeling means the Rio de la Plata, in Argentina."

"Not so fast, Gasp, Rio de la hmmmm." Alex wrestled with his pencil.

"Third, let's find out everything we can about Martin Bormann and any rumors about his treasure and what actually became of him after the war."

"I heard about him on the *Hitler Channel*." Alex laughed, recalling what Gaspar's dad used to call the History Channel.

"Fourth, let's find out what was going on in Buenos Aires around February 7th and July 18th, 1944, just to get a general lay of the land." Gaspar loved Alex quoting his dad's joke.

"Got it boss." Alex never raised his head as he took Gaspar's dictation.

"Fifth, we need to locate the hacienda or ranch of Lahusen. If it exists it must be somewhere in Argentina." Gaspar insisted.

"Maybe we can Google Earth it." Alex suggested.

"Sixth, we need to find out everything we can about Ernst Kaltenbrunner, the Third Reich's chief of the secret police." Gaspar stopped to catch his breath.

"Ya gotta slow down, Gasp. Just look at all this scribble." Alex complained, as he continued writing furiously, "I've practically covered a whole page already."

But Gaspar didn't let up. "Seventh, we need to know today's equivalent of 187,692,400 Deutsch marks, 17,576,500 U.S. dollars, 4,682,500 pounds sterling, 24,976,500 Swiss francs, 8,379,000 gold Dutch florins, 54,963,000 French francs, 17,280,000 Belgian francs and 2,511 kilograms of gold and 4,638 carats of diamonds," he said, reading from his Xerox copies, while scribbling the figures on a pad. "Did you get that, Al? Here," he said ripping off the sheet of paper and handing it to Alex, "can you read my writing?"

"Better than I can read this chicken scratch I've been jotting down. Ya gotta slow down, Gasp." Alex begged again.

"The eighth thing we need to find out is who Bormann's two other partners in crime are, his henchmen. These would be two Germans who committed suicide in Argentina around this time."

Alex was not amused playing stenographer, and pretended not to hear number eight.

"The ninth thing we need to do is look into the mysterious death of Juancito Duarte, Evita Duarte Peron's unfortunate brother, who was presumably laundering this loot for the Nazis on behalf of his sister and brother-in-law."

"Anything else, Gasp?" Alex asked, still scribbling furiously.

"We're not that interested in the 8,000 Argentine passports without signatures or fingerprints, or the 100,000 Argentine identification cards that were signed and sealed by the Argentine police department, also without signatures or fingerprints. But if we can verify any of this, it might come in handy and that will be the tenth item on our list," he said.

"Thank God for small favors," Alex whispered under his breath, still trying to catch up on number nine.

"We will need to learn as much as we can about the Kroops, the Thyssens and the Simenses, Al, and where or if they ended up in Argentina after 1944. We're talking about around 77 people in all. That will be item number eleven ... okay, Al.

"Yes, master." Alex drawled, "Could you repeat number eleven one more time?"

Gaspar ploughed forward, pretending not to hear ... "We also need to learn who Wilfred von Oven is. You can add that to number eleven. Von Oven presumably worked for Joseph Goebbels, Hitler's propaganda chief and wrote for the German newspaper in Buenos Aires. Let's see if we can come up with some of his writings. Then we can get Mr. Gottlieb to translate them for us."

Alex added in the notes, and wiped his forehead. "Any other brilliant ideas, Gasp?" he asked facetiously.

"Let's also learn everything we can about the Vatican and their possible collaboration with the Nazis at this time, especially Pope Pius XII, Bishop Alois Hudal and Monsignor Krunoslav Draganovic. We should also look into the San Girolamo Institute in Rome, and Ante Pavelic. He was the Nazi puppet who ruled Croatia at the time. That's the twelfth order of business for us, Al." Gaspar never looked up from his notes or his list but continued forward.

"This is a mountain of research, Gasp," Alex put down his notebook prematurely. What say we take a break … go for a swim or something and come back to this?"

But Gaspar was deep in thought and hadn't heard a word of Al's reasonable suggestion. "I wonder what a Croat Ustashi is? Apparently 7,250 of them were spirited out of Croatia and into Argentina by these bozos who charged them between $1,000.00 and $1,400.00 each." Gaspar quickly did some calculating on his cell phone. "AL, that would be over $7,250,000.00 back then, more like seventy million today. Item thirteen will be the Croat Ustashi deal. Write that down, bro."

Alex picked up his notebook and went back to work, without further complaint.

"Item number fourteen will be to find out who Altman was and where he stood in the Argentine hierarchy of the Nazi establishment? After that we'll do the same with Rodolfo Freede, who worked for Peron. Let's find out about him, and if he has any family still living in Argentina. Supposedly, according to the *document*, Freede was the son of a businessman and the paymaster for the German spy network in Argentina. Freede was presumably the man in charge of the funds sent in by submarine and it was Freede who Werner Koenecke spied for, as well as the British and the Germans. Koenecke was married to Freede's sister, Lilli, who had been arrested by the Argentine political police in 1944 but later released, on specific orders from Peron.

"How 'bout number fifteen?" Alex was only joking.

"For item number fifteen, we need to look into the activities of Archbishop Alberto Cagliani of the Argentine cities of Rosario and then Buenos Aires, and his association with Pope Pius XII." Gaspar informed him.

"Of course we do," Alex was really getting brain dead, but knew that Gaspar was only just getting started.

"Al, see if you can find any photographic evidence of a U-boat landing in or near Patagonia or the deep south of Argentina during WWII. That's item number sixteen, but we don't have to do this in order. Let's tackle the low-hanging fruit and get the easy stuff out of the way ASAP."

"This is a lot of stuff, Gasp," Alex complained. "When are we gonna have any time for fun like swimmin' and fishin'?"

"This is an adventure, Al. We don't have to do it all at once, but what we're planning here is a road-map which we can follow in our spare time when we're not doing important stuff like goofing off." Gaspar explained. "Now, there are still a few more items we need to research. So let's get this preliminary list out of the way."

"Okay, if you say so. But I'm starting to get mighty hungry." Alex hoped for sympathy.

But Gaspar plowed ahead, "We'll need to learn as much as we can about Eichmann, Mengele and Priebke in order to get to the bottom of this whole business. That is number seventeen on our master list.

At last … the end of the list, Alex breathed a sigh of relief … *too early*.

"Number eighteen will be to find out as much as we can about Newt Frankhauser and his connection to Hitler, The Ahnenerbe and the mysterious *Necronomicon*. We'll need to look into the Ahnenerbe in detail and find out about their secret headquarters in the Murg Valley, wherever that is? Make a note, Al. You're in charge of the maps and *Google Earth* on this project. Go to the Murg Valley now and tell me where it is!" Gaspar prodded his friend into action.

"This should keep us busy for a while, Al." Gaspar joked, looking over the many pages of scribbled notes his pal had assembled. "Tell you what, Al. You take the first ten and I'll take the last eleven and we should get this research done in no time, like a month or two at the most," he chuckled. But right now let's head to the kitchen and rustle up something to eat, I'm starving … and then we could go for a swim … wha-da-ya think?"

"I think I should have thought of that myself … " Alex joked good naturedly.

The two boys headed to the kitchen, where they found the room thankfully deserted. Rummaging through the old icebox they found bread and peanut butter and raspberry jam and began immediately preparing sandwiches.

"Have you got any bacon?" Alex asked seriously.

"Yeah, we have bacon." Gaspar answered, pulling a pack out of the refrigerator.

"We can't have peanut butter and jelly without bacon." Alex insisted.

"No problem, Al." Gaspar assured his friend, pulling out a skillet and dumping the entire package of Farmer John into the pan. "This will be ready in a jiffy. You keep making the sandwiches, and grab a couple of cokes, and get a couple of glasses and put some ice in them." Gaspar instructed his friend, from his position at the stove.

Soon the boys were back in the office, each carrying a dish of sandwiches, and a glass bubbling with Coca-Cola.

They sat across from each other at Uncle Charlie's big partner's desk, which Gaspar had outfitted with two computers, a printer and scanner so they could work together on homework and other imaginative projects they elected to fill their time with.

"So, Gaspar, help me out. You think by following some clues written a long time ago, we might actually find a cache of Nazi gold in Argentina?" Alex asked, all joking aside.

"Of course, Al. Why not, and even if we don't find any gold, it will be an adventure. Maybe we'll even learn some lessons from the events of the last century that we can apply to the present."

"What I want to know is how you plan to take possession of the treasure, after we find it?" Alex asked, mystified. "How will you get it out of wherever it is and back to La Rinconada?" Alex asked, in his most serious, conspiratorial tone of voice.

"I've been asking myself the same question, Al, and I haven't come up with an answer yet." Gaspar admitted meekly. "All we have here," he said, picking up his notes, "is the beginning of an adventure. Right now we need to map it out, and learn what we can. Then when Christmas vacation rolls around, if we're lucky, maybe we could head to wherever and check some of these facts or fictions out."

"We're gonna go to Argentina?" Alex asked, dumbfounded.

"Well we're not gonna find Nazi treasure here on Perdido Isle, are we? So we'll need to follow the clues down to Buenos Aires or wherever our quest takes us." Gaspar's commitment was complete.

"That sounds reasonable," Alex commented. "I'll get started on the first ten items, and get back to you … but this project isn't taking precedence over our other activities … is it?"

"You heard me loud and clear, Al. Which means, we better get on our bikes and meet the gang down at the ol' swimmin' hole, before they think we've deserted them," Gaspar chuckled.

CHAPTER 25

ENTER THE VRILERINNEN

THE BIG NIGHT HAD ARRIVED. NOTHING LIKE IT HAD EVER TAKEN PLACE ON PERDIDO ISLE BEFORE. INTEREST in the subject of Vril Power was so intense that the venue had to be moved from the clubhouse at Villa Gaspar to the big ballroom of the Grand Hotel Floride. The room held a thousand people, and there were still many clambering for tickets the day of the big event. Interest was not limited to just those living on the island. Reservations had been received from all over the United States, and from as far away as New Delhi, Tibet, Buenos Aires, St. Petersburg, Berlin, and of course, Paris, London, and Rome. Even the Vatican was sending a special envoy to sit in on the discussion.

Gaspar couldn't believe all the fuss, and hoped he hadn't bitten off more than he could chew. The guest speaker and her posse had flown in from Buenos Aires, and were comfortably ensconced in one of the biggest suites at the hotel. He had made sure that her suite was filled with rubrum lilies and pots of flowering orchids. It had been stocked with exotic fruits, juices, and of course lots of vintage French champagne. He had consulted Uncle Charlie on all of these arrangements, who had happily advised him.

The presentation was scheduled for eight o'clock, and by 7:30 all the best seats in the house had been taken except for those roped off in the front row, which Gaspar had reserved for his friends. Elvira, Peter, Brewster and Mrs. Crabtree were in the front row. Karen, Frank, Lamar, Captain Morgan, Sergeant O'Malley and Lieutenant Jacobson were across the aisle. Craig Cadawalader, Felix, Angela and Alex were sitting Kevin, Sancho, Mark, Pat, and Mrs. Hobart, along side them.

When the clock struck eight, Gaspar stepped out onto the stage to thunderous applause. "Ladies and gentlemen," he welcomed the crowd, "I'm pleased to present the first in a series of talks about esoteric subjects, which I hope you will find enlightening. The purpose of these evenings is not to indoctrinate, but to expose all of us to new ideas, which we may not have considered important or relevant to our sheltered lives here in our own garden of paradise, Perdido Isle. Please join me in welcoming my special guest, the medium and leader of the Vrilerinnen, Maria Orsic, and the four beautiful young ladies of the Vril Gesellschaft." The audience exploded when the five gorgeous creatures with long blond hair floated onto the stage wearing diaphanous gowns. Taking a bow, they stood on each side of Gaspar, smiling at the audience, before sitting demurely to the left and right of the two chairs in the center of the stage which Gaspar and Maria Orsic soon occupied.

"Welcome, Vrilerinne. We are very pleased to have you here tonight on Perdido Isle. Gaspar spoke directly to Maria Orsic. "Tell us where you come from, and what Vril Power is and why Vril should be important to us," Gaspar implored the Amazonian.

Gaspar nearly fell out of his chair when the mighty Vrilerinne answered, "We come from the planet Aldebaran, and we are here to save the earth."

The audience sat stunned, motionless, silent.

Quickly Gaspar asked the next question. "But you live in Buenos Aires, Argentina?"

"Yes, we have lived there for many years, since the end of the last world war to be exact. We moved there from Berlin, via Antarctica." The Vrilerinne threw in, cryptically.

"You mean your parents moved you there in the late 1940s, after World War II?" Gaspar asked, somewhat confused.

"No, our parents are still on Aldebaran. When we moved to Buenos Aires with many other Thule, it was under duress," Maria smiled sweetly, tossing her long blond hair.

The audience collectively inhaled, and held their breaths.

"But surely you must have been infants when you moved to Argentina in 1945?" Gaspar asked the obviously twenty-something-year-old woman, while grasping at straws.

"No, in earth years we are each about 175 years old, but by Aldebaran standards we are still considered young women." Maria smiled at the Vrilerinnen.

The audience collectively exhaled, in a torrent of disbelieving murmurs.

In an attempt to normalize the conversation, Gaspar said, "Maria, please introduce us to the Vrilerinnen," as he motioned to the other gorgeous creatures seated around him on the stage. "Tell us, if it is not too impolite, each of their ages."

"This is Traute and this is Sigrun, she motioned to Gaspar's right, and this is Gudrun and next is Heike, she said pointing to his left, while motioning to each of the ladies. We are all about the same age, give or take a few years," she giggled.

"You certainly are beautiful. You each have a very distinctive personal style and way of dressing," Gaspar acknowledged.

"We wear our hair long because our hair serves as our cosmic antenna. Our hair is like a conduit that helps us communicate with the universe and with beings from beyond earth's limited galaxy."

A collective gasp emerged from the audience, when Heike imparted this information.

Gaspar took a deep breath and jumped in with both feet. "So tell me, Vril Damen, just what or who are you saving the world from?"

"From itself ... and from corrupt governments who want to keep their people suppressed and enslaved and dependent on expensive and often times dangerous energy sources. We're here to tell you there's a simpler way to power this planet," Traute explained.

"How long, in earth years have you been on this planet?" Gaspar asked. "What year exactly did you get here?"

"We five Vril Damen came to earth in 1919, right after your disastrous First World War. We came to save the earth then, and as you all know, our reason for coming here is still not accomplished," Traute said, sternly.

"One of the first contacts we made after we arrived on earth was with the leaders of the German Thule, Vril and Black Sun Societies." Vrilerinne Maria Orsic took over. "At that meeting I received telepathic messages from my own Aldebaran solar system, 68 light years away. Aldebaran is in the constellation of Taurus, for those of you familiar with star maps," Maria explained, as a map of the solar system appeared on the big screen, behind them.

"What were the transmissions about?" Gaspar asked the question that the entire audience wanted to know.

"They were very strange, but easily understood by the assembled audience in 1919." Maria expounded. "It seems that when I spoke to the audience that night, without knowing it, I spoke in tongues. This is not unusual for a medium like myself, but it still came as a surprise to me. You can imagine how disconcerting it was to the audience that night since they had never experienced such a phenomenon before. The words came out of my mouth in a man's voice, speaking the ancient coded language of a secret order of the German Knights Templar. After I had imparted those words of wisdom, which were merely a cordial greeting from a disembodied entity, a second transmission came out in an even more ancient eastern tongue. A Babylonian scholar in the audience associated my words with the Thule, and recognized my words as ancient Sumerian."

"Can you tell us what the words you spoke were?" Gaspar asked. "Tell us please, the gist of the second transmission?"

"Yes, I can. Sigrun, on your left, helped me with the Sumerian translation. Apparently what I was telling the assembled group was how to build a circular flight machine. What you would call a flying saucer."

The audience in the ballroom sucked in a collective deep breath, and then exhaled in whispers to each other that varied from, *what the heck* to *oh my God*.

Jackpot … Gaspar couldn't believe his good fortune … *or did he mean crackpot?* "You've got to be kidding me!" was all that came out of his mouth.

"No, if you would show the next slide, please," Maria said to the audio-visual technician in charge of the presentation. Suddenly up on the big screen behind them, a diagram appeared showing exactly what Maria was talking about.

"Did you draw that?" Gaspar asked, amazed.

"No, Gudrun drew it, while Sigrun translated what I was saying. It is a form of automatic drawing that Gudrun enjoys. It is as unique to her, as my ability to intercept transmissions from other planets, is to me," Maria informed them.

"What is the motivation for the Aldebaran civilization's desire to assist us here on Earth?" Gaspar asked innocently.

"When we arrived here after the Great War, we felt that there was an economic disparity in earth's cultures, which seemed to be the problem that was perpetuating all the world's violent conflicts. My people reasoned that we could help the earth by offering our *free energy* technologies, which would help the people of earth create affordable mass transportation machines and power new industries founded on innovative ideas, which would help promote success and prosperity worldwide. Imagine a peaceful interaction between former warring nations. The end of violence and war, the end of death and destruction, jealousy, rivalry and hatred, replaced with industries based on scientific principles of free energy. This was our plan, and we haven't yet given up on our charge. Back at the turn of the century, the idea of free energy resonated with the Thule and Vril Societies. Their dream had always been for a Utopian world, a return to Eden, a *new world order* created with the help of alternative science," Maria finished.

"Tell us about the next slide which is just now up on the screen," Gaspar begged. He loved that the audience was sitting quietly wide-eyed, eating this up.

"This is a design for a perpetual motion engine, which once started, needs never to stop running. It has only two moving parts, uses no fossil fuel to run, as it is operated almost entirely by magnetism. Once started it will never ever stop, unless it is purposefully shut down, which is possible but not probable. The longer this engine runs, the more energy it creates. The possibilities are limitless as to its power to run entire cities, countries, and all types of machinery. Imagine being able to harness such energy. Imagine the Earth and all of its commercial manufacturing enterprises powered by such machines, from the lowliest sewing machine to the most complicated computerized internet grid. I am talking about an endless supply of free, clean, non-polluting power, which is everyman's dream. It is within your reach, if dark international government forces were not keeping our Aldebaran gift to you, a secret."

"Have these ideas been tested or your drawings been looked at by any Earth scientists and if so, who were they and why aren't these machines in use today?" Gaspar questioned.

"Dr. W. O. Schumann and his associates from the University of Munich, made a study of our plans, and actually created a working model. They knew that the plans I had channeled, and that Gudrun had drawn, actually contained viable physics. By 1922 they actually had a working perpetual motion engine, as well as an anti-gravity flying machine in full operation."

"At what point were the Germans ready to try a manned test flight of the anti-gravity flying machine?" Gaspar interjected.

"In 1934 the first manned test flight, of what the Germans called the RFZ-1, took place. I would be lying if I told you it was an amazing success. Lothar Waiz, the heroic German World War I ace, took the prototype up but it wobbled out of control at an altitude of only 150 feet. When he landed the disc, he barely managed to escape with his life, before it spun out of control, ripping itself to pieces.

"Did the Germans continue with their experiments in flying discs?" Gaspar wondered.

"Oh, yes. Before the year was out, they had made another vastly-improved version, the RFZ-2, which was five meters in diameter." Maria told the enthralled audience, "The test flight was very, very successful and so the military stepped up the development of the flying discs, as a division of the army, that would be Division SS E-IV."

"So the German Army got their hands on the invention and that was the end of that." Gaspar shrugged.

"Well, this was indeed our downfall," Heike sighed. "We thought the Germans would want to use our knowledge to better their people through economics, rather than war. They took our peaceful invention and turned it into a tool for destruction, subjugation and horror."

"How exactly does a flying saucer … fly?" Gaspar moved them along.

"It's nothing more than a child's toy, like a top or a gyroscope," Traute spoke up. "Two circular rims spinning counter-clockwise to each other create an anti-gravity effect, just like the one written about in the Old Testament, when the prophet Ezekiel took off in his fiery chariot. That was basically a wheel within a wheel."

Gaspar wanted to jump out of his chair with excitement, but somehow continued with the interview. He was relieved that the audience seemed to be as much in awe of these crazy ladies as he was.

"Tell me, truthfully, Maria, was what the Hebrew patriarch witnessed actually a flying machine from Aldebaran?"

"You are a very prescient fellow, Mr. Brown, and the first to make that connection. Yes, we have been visiting Earth since Adam and Eve's banishment from Paradise, hoping to show your people the light and the way back to Eden. It could all be so easy if your governments and big businesses would just step aside and free the people from the chains of high-priced energy. We can show you the way, but what good is direction without desire." Maria shook her head in disillusionment. "The problem with *free energy* is that it is FREE. Since nobody can make any money off of it, nobody is interested in giving it to the people. It is criminal, but true." She finished up.

With that, several vintage photographs of German flying saucers came up on the screen, all of them images which none of the assembled Perdidians had ever seen before.

"Tell us about Hitler. What role did he play in this cover up?" Gaspar wanted to know.

"We met with Hitler personally on more than one occasion. Although he professed to us his interest in creating a world of cosmic harmony, he then turned around and sent his Panzer tanks and heavily-armed soldiers into Poland in 1939, thus precipitating the disastrous and positively destructive Second World War."

"What exactly is Vril?" Gaspar feared the answer, but had to ask it.

"It's very simple, Mr. Brown. It's what we have been talking about all evening. Vril is free energy. It is Vril Power that levitates the flying saucers. It is Vril Power that motivates the perpetual motion engines."

"I understand," Gaspar said. "It is all very simple, and yet so complicated, because your secret gift has somehow been subverted by powers greater than all of us."

"That is correct. The nations of the earth, first wanting to use Vril Power for conquest, subverted it in exchange for gold from the petroleum, coal, hydroelectric and nuclear providers. Those industries still control the Earth's highly profitable energy sources and are the ones that have kept Vril Power hidden away, and lost to humanity."

"What you are telling us is that you, unfortunately, chose the wrong people to deal with in the first place," Gaspar said.

"Correct. We thought the broken German people, after World War One, would be open to the idea of free energy to help revive their bankrupt economy, spreading prosperity throughout the world, by example. But then with the rise of Hitler and his dreams of world domination, our Vril Power was usurped by the military, who used it for evil instead of good. Once the Luftwaffe got their hands on it, the Allied nations couldn't help but want Vril Power too, in order to combat fire with fire. We refused to give the Allies our secret. Not because we were against them, but because we didn't want Vril to go viral through warfare. Of course, in the end, the Allies received the secret from the conquered Germans. They then hid it away at the request of the energy companies that have dominated the world since the end of the war."

"So it all started with the Luftwaffe. Tell us about their involvement," Gaspar implored.

"It was the evil aero-technical unit of the Luftwaffe who ultimately developed the V-7 hybrid that combined anti-gravity power developed with our methods and conventional turbojet propulsion systems. That these would be used for destructive purposes horrified us and hurt us, for we Vrilerians are sensitive creatures," Traute cried.

"It's hard to believe that Hitler wasn't interested in the free energy technology that you handed him on a silver platter," Gaspar scoffed.

"Don't get me wrong. Hitler and his SS E-IV unit took it upon themselves to develop free energy propulsion. Our technology was Hitler's dream come true. What he wasn't interested in was using our technology for the economic good of his people. That is what hurt us," Traute stormed.

"It's hard to believe, all these years later, that the Germans had the technology for free energy, and that the Americans and Russians got their hands on it after the war? Can you convince us of this truth." Gaspar asked, disbelievingly.

"Oh yes," said Sigrun, "most definitely! The United States and the Russians know our secrets, absolutely. The technology was proven in 1941 when the German Vril-2 levitation craft was used on transatlantic reconnaissance missions. There was even a more sophisticated model.

which the Germans called the RFZ-2, which used their own Schumman-Levitator drive for vertical lift. It was developed using our technology, but with additions by Dr. Schumman, which in our opinion were not newer or better than our own inventions. We felt that if it made them feel more a part of the solution, then who were we to say anything. You see, we never gave up hope that they would come to their senses and see the evil of their ways."

"So the newer model was unimpressive?" Gaspar pondered.

"No, I wouldn't say unimpressive, but possibly over thought," Sigrun continued. "When the levitator drive was activated, the saucer worked just like one of our own craft. You have probably heard reports of UFOs and how their visible contours always appear blurred, and that at night they appear to have a luminous ionization of colors which change from orange to green and blue to white. Those colors can be attributed to the engine's acceleration levels. It was also noted at the time, the ability of the craft to radically make 90 degree turns at full speed, all traits which are characteristic in all UFO sightings today."

"So basically, your big beef with us earthlings is that the world governments have turned your free energy from something that could benefit all men, into something that can be used only to destroy them." Gaspar hit the nail on the head.

"That is correct, Mr. Brown. You have summed up our complaints in a sentence," Maria agreed. "It started when the Reich turned the success of the RFZ-2 into a single-pilot combat model. Then to add insult to injury, after the war ended, the other world governments stepped in and confiscated our technology for their own military purposes. After that, the peaceful intent of the Aldebaran's levitation technology and perpetual motion energy systems had been hidden away, and lost to the benefit of all men," Maria bemoaned.

"Why haven't we heard of Vril before? Why do you think our government is keeping this marvelous free energy from us?" Gaspar asked.

"These things we talk about have all become top secret, classified information. You can believe us when we tell you that all of this is the truth," Maria insisted. It's the world governments who don't think their people are ready for the truth, when in fact, you are ready right now for Vril Power to be unleashed. With Vril Power in place, you can start cleaning up your environment, and banking money instead of paying it out because of oil spills and nuclear cleanups. Imagine the billions that could be saved and used for more munificent purposes … like education, the arts, infrastructure repairs and other projects for the common good."

"Tell us just a little bit more about that RFZ-2 fighter," Gaspar insisted. "I know of no reports of battles between flying saucers, and regular RAF or U.S. Air Force fighter planes."

"There was one very significant altercation between the United States Air Force, the RAF and the German saucer fleet. It was in 1944 after the Americans had unleashed a deadly bombing raid on a ball bearing plant at Schweinfurt. On the defensive, Germany moved in its own secret weapons. Within hours, a squadron of fifteen German saucers had downed 150 British and American bombers. That was one quarter of the entire Allied bomber contingent. Even after that horrible victory, the crumbling Reich still lacked enough saucers to make a difference in the war against Allied fighting superiority," Maria finished up.

Heike took up the tale where Maria had left off. "The Vril-1 was able to reach speeds of 12,000 km/h and could make sharp right-angle turns at full speed without causing adverse G-effects on the navigator. You have to understand, when you fly in a self-contained vehicle capable of creating its own gravitational field, there is no sense of motion or inertia."

"But tell them about the RFZ-2, Heike," Maria jumped in. "If the Vril-1 could reach 12,000 km/h, the RFZ-2 could reach speeds twice as fast with the same agile abilities to turn, bank and zigzag."

"Don't forget the other ships that the Germans built between 1941 and 1944. Remember the awful Haunebu. That was the real heavy hitter of the Reich's saucer fleet,"

Gudrun put in her two cents. "Subsequent levitation craft advances between 1941 and 1944 spawned the "Haunebu" series, the heavy hitters of the Reich's saucer fleet."

"But it was the development of the powerful tachyon magneto-gravitic drives and the Thule tachyonators, which were basically large spheres of vertically rotating mercury, that allowed the designers to dream up their new horrifying 75 foot diameter armored saucer ships. These machines of destruction were equipped with Panzer tank cannon turrets, mounted to the undersides of the crafts." Traute expounded on the death platters.

"Those were nothing," Sigrun chimed in. "There were other craft designed with klystron laser cannons, which were far deadlier at longer distances than the mere death platters."

"So what came next, Maria?" Gaspar asked, knowing that they were running out of time, and hoping that the stock-still audience would not soon be getting restless.

"Around Christmas of 1943, I received more transmissions from Aldebaran," recalled Maria Orsic. "These transmissions revealed the presence of two habitable planets orbiting Aldebaran. People from the ancient Mesopotamian civilization of Sumeria had been taken there thousands of years earlier, to join up with even earlier colonies of Aldebaran explorers, who had also settled there. It was at the time of these later transmissions that I realized that the Aldebaran language is identical to that of the Sumerians and both languages are phonetically similar to that of spoken German."

"That's very interesting, Maria," Gaspar commented, while making a mental note to find recordings of German and Sumarian readings so that he could compare them phonetically to see if Maria was on to something or not. He also didn't think it was a bad idea to study some Sumerian phrases in the event that he ever ended up on Aldebaran.

"It was also revealed to me at that time," Maria continued, "that a dimensional channel, like a wormhole, existed as a connection between our two solar systems."

"Did anyone try to find out if the wormhole theory was actual?" Gaspar asked.

"Yes, the Germans took the information I gave them. I still had hopes that they would use my information for good, but alas, nothing was to come of all of this, as history has recorded. It was in January 1944, because of information received through me, that the Germans tried to send one of their Vril-7 saucers through this dimensional channel in hopes of securing additional military assistance from Aldebaran. The fools could never get it through their heads that ours was a peaceful planet, and that we had actually failed in our efforts to bring peace to earth. I really think the Germans thought we had been sent by God to present them with more and more devastating arms."

"Tell us what happened to the Germans' flight to Aldebaran?" Gaspar questioned, not wanting to be left hanging for another moment.

"Oh, that was a failure," Maria said, nonchalantly. "A disaster really. The Vril-7 returned to base damaged beyond recognition, as if it had been traveling for centuries, which perhaps it had. But to us, here on earth, the craft had only just left a few hours before it returned to base."

"How can you explain that?" Gaspar was all ears.

"The ship had to have entered a time-space continuum," Maria stated boldly. "The venture resulted in near disaster. The Vril-7 returned with its hull aged, as if it had been flying for 200 years and its surface was badly damaged in several places. The body of the pilot was found inside, mummified, as if it had been dead for at least 200 years as well."

"So what happened to all the German flying saucers after the war?" Gaspar asked. "They certainly couldn't have all been destroyed in fire fights?"

"Well, this is another story," Gudrun reported. "It revolves around a German officer named Hans Kammler, who was a protégé of Heinrich Himmler. Kammler had a reputation for being able to get any job done well, and in a hurry. In the meantime, Kammler had accumulated so much power within the SS Elite that it was said he wielded as much power, if not more than Hitler himself."

"That's a lot of power," Gaspar commented. "And we're not talking about Vril Power either," he joked to the amusement of his audience.

"By 1945," Gudrun told them, "Kammler was in charge of all the top secret SS projects that were missile or aircraft related. That of course included the Vril saucer fleet. The saucers soon became one of Kammler's foremost interests. A shrewd man, Kammler quickly constructed a special projects facility at the South Pole. On April 17, 1945 Kammler left Germany and took us, the Vrilerinnen with him. He got out of Germany in the nick of time, with the five of us as his captives, on board a behemoth six-engine Junkers 390 Amerika bomber. We were bound for an unknown destination, which ended up to be Buenos Aires, Argentina," Gudrun smiled weakly at the audience.

Maria picked up the story where Gudrun left off. "Although we transmitted brain waves to our home base asking for help, no rescue from Aldebaran was forthcoming. Once in Argentina, we were transported to a secret underground lair in Neuschwabenland, Antarctica, near the South Pole, where we were amazed to find a huge facility housing thousands of workers and elite Germans. What we saw being built there was a massive 250-foot diameter Haunebu III dreadnought armed with four triple-gun cannons, housed within heavy caliber naval turrets. We quickly ascertained that this ship was ready and fully capable of space flight. Kammler told us that he wanted us on board when the ship took off for Aldebaran."

"Shortly thereafter, we heard over the radio that the Russian, British and American armies were relentlessly advancing on the German heartland. Because of the inevitable end of the war … supplies, scientists and saucer components were being steadily evacuated from Europe by U-boats to secret enclaves in Germany's Antarctic colony—Neuschwabenland. Just one month prior to the Haunebu III's completion I sent a telepathic message to all the members of the Vril Society still in Germany, simply stating "we are already gone, none of us are staying". That was the last time that I or the Vrilerinnen were to hear or see anything of the outside world for many years. As Kammler's captives, we were forced to collaborate with him. It was many years before we could effect our escape from that secret underground Antarctic lair. But we did manage, shortly after Kammler's death. After Kammler died, there was a lot of confusion and lack of leadership. We managed to get out with another group of dissatisfied elites, while the security was lax. We have been living together ever since in a large house in Buenos Aires, as guests of the Argentine government. We continue to communicate with our home base on Aldebaran. We hope to expose the benefits of free energy to Earth to make it a better place for all of us to live, not a more dangerous place to live."

"Thank you very much, Vrilerinne Maria Orsic for opening our eyes to Vril, and thank you Vrilerinnen," Gaspar said, standing up and motioning to all five of his guests. We look forward to the future of Free Vril Energy, the history and promise of which you have shown us so clearly tonight."

As the Vrilerinne and her four Vrilerinnen exited the stage followed by Gaspar, the entire audience stood up in thunderous applause.

Later, on the ride back to La Rinconada with Elvira, Peter and Alex, Gaspar admitted, "Those gals were nutty, but what they had to say was powerful. When I questioned them back stage, they told me, "If you can think of it, Gaspar, we guarantee you it has already been done. Your government already knows how to do it based on the knowledge they have received from Aldebaran. They're just not ready to share it with you yet." He finished up his thought, "You know, Al, it's like the internet. The government got the technology from the Aldebarans a long time ago and knew how to do that for years and years. And then one day they decided people could handle it and a whole new era started, and it was basically for free. Now our eyes have been opened to free energy, and it's up to us to make sure it happens before it's too late! That was Gaspar's last words on the subject before the car turned into the gates of La Rinconada. But deep down inside, he knew his quest to discover the mystery of the jeweled dagger was far from over and he was already formulating a plan on how to accomplish that goal. But there was something else praying on his mind and that was the *Necronomicon* and its possible whereabouts. Little did Gaspar know that in just a few weeks, he would be dragging his friends into yet another adventure of a lifetime, which would make the mystery of the Seminole Spring look like child's play as they tackle *The Mystery of the Necronomicon*.

Made in the USA
Columbia, SC
16 February 2019